STRAWBERRY CRUSH

STRAWBERRY CRUSH

Jean Ure

HarperCollins *Children's Books*

First published in Great Britain by HarperCollins *Children's Books* 2016
HarperCollins *Children's Books* is a division of HarperCollins*Publishers* Ltd,
HarperCollins Publishers
1 London Bridge Street
London SE1 9GF
The HarperCollins *Children's Books* website address is
www.harpercollins.co.uk

1

ISBN 978-0-00-755396-9

Typeset by Palimpsest Book Production Ltd, Falkirk, Stirlingshire

Printed and bound in England by
Clays Ltd, St Ives plc

CHAPTER ONE

I was there the day it all started: the day Maya fell off her bike straight into the arms of Jake Harper.

Well, not actually *straight* into his arms. But practically right in front of him.

It was the start of the summer term and we were on our way back from school, cycling up Layhams Hill, two abreast cos there wasn't that much traffic around. We were busy talking – as usual! – when Maya suddenly gave this great wobble, lurched into the kerb and slid with a startled squawk over the handlebars.

I have to admit it looked pretty dramatic, but I wasn't particularly alarmed. Maya was always coming off her bike. Unlike me, who is quite chunky and solid, Maya is a tiny little creature, almost elfin, but she's the one who is forever tripping over her own feet or shutting her fingers in the door. Still, we were both wearing helmets so I reckoned she couldn't have done that much damage.

I skidded to a halt and turned back to look at her. "You OK?"

I was sure that she was. She'd already started to pick herself up, so obviously nothing was broken and I couldn't see any blood. But then a car pulled in on the other side of the road, the driver's door was flung open and Jake came rushing across.

"Do you need any help?"

Honestly, it was like some kind of magic spell. Some kind of automatic reaction. Before I knew it, Maya had sunk back on to the pavement and burst into heart-rending sobs. I felt so embarrassed! I mean, it was just so *obvious*.

"Are you OK?" Jake had squatted down beside her and put an arm round her shoulders. "That looked painful!"

Oh, please, I thought, *don't encourage her!*

"Have you done any damage?"

Maya, weeping piteously, held out one of her hands. She'd grazed it on the pavement, but it was hardly gushing blood.

I shook my head. Un-be-liev-able! Shameless, in fact. Talk about a drama queen.

"Best have that looked at," said Jake. "You could have got some dirt in it. Let's get you into the car and I'll give you a lift home."

With the help of Jake's supporting arm, Maya tottered feebly to her feet.

"Can you manage to walk?"

She sniffed, heroically. "I'll try."

"Well, take it slowly. Mattie, do you want to grab her bike?"

I thought, *Oh, if I must.*

"We can put yours in, too, if you like. I might as well give you both a lift. You're just round the corner from each other, aren't you?"

I was about to say, rather ungraciously, that I didn't need a lift, we were only five minutes away, but then I thought, who in their right mind would turn down a ride in a car with the great Jake Harper? Just about the coolest boy in the school!

I wheeled both bikes across the road, pulling a face behind Maya's back as I did so. She was really playing things for all they were worth!

"Easy does it," said Jake, helping her into the car. Needless to say, she got the front seat. I had to sit crammed into the back, against the bikes, with my legs all curled up and handlebars digging into me.

"OK?" said Jake.

I said, "Fine!" I didn't want him thinking I was as big a wimp as Maya. A little bit of discomfort was nothing to *me*.

"I'd better go in first," I said, "and tell your mum."

Maya's mum tends to panic. Although she and my mum are twins they are *so* not identical. Mum is really down to earth and practical; she takes things in her stride. I think I am a bit like her. Auntie Megs, on the other hand, is more of a nervous type. I guess that's where Maya gets it from. I knew if I didn't go ahead and break the news, *gently*, Auntie Megs would immediately think Maya was at death's door.

But then, omigod! As I uncurled my legs and clambered my way out of the car I saw that Jake had already gone round to the passenger side and was actually preparing to *carry* Maya up to the house. It was like something out of a cheesy romance movie. I do actually quite enjoy cheesy romance movies – sometimes – but this was just embarrassing! Maya was being *poor little fragile me*, and Jake was falling for it. Maybe it made him feel… I don't know… manly. I know some boys like to feel that, just as some girls like to play helpless. I have too much pride! I'd have managed to stagger indoors without any help even if I'd had to hop on one leg. But that is just me.

"Let me go first!"

Rudely I pushed past them and raced up to the door. Auntie Megs must have been keeping watch – waiting, in her anxious way, for Maya to arrive home – because the door flew open even before I got there.

"Mattie!" shrieked Auntie Megs. "What's happened?"

"Nothing; it's nothing," I said. "She fell off her bike, but she's perfectly OK!"

Not that it looked like it, with Jake cradling her in his arms.

"Honestly," I said, "she's just grazed her hand. Nothing to worry about."

But Auntie Megs worries about everything. She has

this long list of rules that are designed to keep you safe. Rule No. 1, never go anywhere near a tree if you are out in a storm in case you get struck by lightning. Rule No. 2, never get into the first or the last carriage on a train in case the train gets hit by another train. Rule No. 3, never walk under a piece of scaffolding in case it collapses on top of you. The list is endless! So naturally, seeing a limp body being carried up the garden path she feared the worst. To be fair, I expect any mum would have. Even mine might have been a little bit alarmed. It was so over the top!

Maya was obviously basking in it, and I guess Jake was, too. He carried her through the house and set her down, very gently, on the sofa.

"There you go! No broken bones, but it was a nasty tumble."

Nasty *tumble*? Whoever uses the word tumble? Unless they're talking about a tumble dryer? Unless... maybe he had chosen the word specially, so as not to cause too much alarm. Maybe he'd thought if he said "a nasty fall" Auntie Meg would fly into one of her panics.

She was going to fly into a panic anyway. As soothingly as I could I said that Maya had just come off her bike. Like she hadn't come off it a dozen times before.

"I knew this would happen!" cried Auntie Megs. "I've said all along, you shouldn't be cycling."

"We always wear our helmets," I said.

"I don't care, it's still not safe! You could still get a concussion."

I tried exchanging glances with Jake, but he was too busy concentrating on Maya and didn't notice. I waited while Auntie Megs fussed about, checking for concussion by holding up a finger and telling Maya to follow it, then decided I'd had enough. I was used to Auntie Megs getting in a flap but I never thought I'd see Jake going all soft and drippy. Jake Harper was one of *the* coolest people on the planet! He was not only a prefect, he was also captain of the school football team.

But Auntie Megs does cleaning for his mum so probably, maybe, he felt duty-bound to show concern. Just not that much! I felt like screaming, "There's nothing wrong with her!"

"I'll go and get the bikes," I said.

"Hang on!" Jake came after me. "I'll give you a hand. Let me just take Maya's in for her then I'll run you home."

Well! How could I say no? I am *not* someone that goes soft and drippy but there's this girl that lives in my road, Linzi Baxter, that reckons all the boys fancy her. She's in Year Eight along with me and Maya and is a really tiresome sort of person. With any luck she might be coming back from school in time to see me getting out of the car. *And* see who was driving it. That would give her something to think about! There aren't many boys at our school get to drive their own cars. She'd certainly never gone out with one.

I suppose that is a bit shallow, really, but girls like Linzi, always so full of themselves, really do my head in.

"I'll just go and tell Maya I'm off," I said.

Jake came back in with me, wheeling the bike.

"Maya," I said, "we're going."

"All right."

She'd been sitting up but immediately flopped back down again, giving us this little trembly smile from out of her pile of cushions.

"See you tomorrow," I said.

A sort of sigh escaped her. It was like "Mmmmmm…"

"I'm not having her back on that bike," said Auntie Megs. "My nerves can't stand it."

"OK." I shrugged. "We'll take the bus."

It isn't any use trying to reason with Auntie Megs; it just gets her even more flustered. But I grumbled about it in the car.

"It's such a drag, hanging around for the bus! Cycling's perfectly safe, as long as you wear a helmet. It's not like we're in London! I could understand it if we were in London. But I mean, out here it's, like – well! It's just fields and stuff. Auntie Megs makes such a fuss!"

"I guess you can understand it," said Jake. "Maya's quite a delicate little thing, isn't she?"

Oh, yuck!

"Not especially," I said. "She just looks like she is. She's actually quite tough."

"No one would ever think it," said Jake.

I felt like telling him that if he hadn't been there Maya would simply have picked herself up and got back on her bike. She wouldn't have had much choice, cos I wouldn't have fussed and flapped over her! But I didn't say anything, cos I didn't want him thinking I was cold and heartless. It's just that what with being born only weeks apart, and with our mums being twins, we've been brought up almost like sisters, so I really do know her inside out. It is only emotionally, like Auntie Megs, that she is a bit fragile, which is why I always feel I have to be there for her. Sometimes some of my friends get a bit impatient and say why do I bother, but it's like a sort of duty. I couldn't just turn my back. It was the only reason I'd agreed to get the bus instead of carrying on cycling by myself.

Linzi Baxter was unfortunately nowhere to be seen as we turned into Orchard Close. I guess it was a bit too much to hope for. She is the sort of person that is always there when you don't want her to be and nowhere to be seen when you feel like doing a bit of showing off. Probably served me right. Showing off is very pathetic. I don't usually stoop to it. *Unlike Linzi.*

I told Jake thanks for the lift, and he said no problem.

"Let me get your bike out for you… there you go!"

I hovered for a few seconds as he drove away, but there were still no signs of life from Linzi's house. Unless perhaps she was peering from behind the curtain. I wouldn't put it past her!

I wheeled my bike round the back and went in through the kitchen. Mum was on the phone. I heard her say, "Well, keep an eye on her. I'm sure she'll be fine."

"Was that Auntie Megs?" I said. "Telling you about Maya? She just fell off her bike; she didn't do any damage. Well, apart from scraping her hand. Nothing to get fussed about."

"No, I'm sure you're right, but you know what your auntie's like," said Mum. "What's this I hear about Jake rushing to the rescue?"

"He was just driving past," I said. "He saw her come off so he stopped to help."

"Actually carried her over the threshold, so I hear!"

"Yes. Well." I pulled a face. "It was all done for show. He didn't have to."

"Still, good for him," said Mum. "It's nice to know the days of chivalry are not completely over."

"But, Mum," I cried, "it was so embarrassing! She got all silly and swoony and burst into tears. She wouldn't have done it if Jake hadn't been there."

"Don't be too hard on her," urged Mum. "She's going through a really tough time right now. So's your Auntie

Megs. They're both missing Uncle Kev and you can't blame them for being worried about him."

I sighed. "I know. I do try…"

Maya's dad, my Uncle Kev, is what *my* dad calls selfish and unreliable. Dad doesn't have much patience with him. Mum, more kindly, says he's just a bit eccentric. Actually, if you ask me he is *very* eccentric. I do love him, cos he's also funny and warm-hearted and generous, but I can see why Dad accuses him of being selfish. He is one of those people that can't ever seem to settle to anything. He was a milkman for a little while, but that didn't work out, so then he worked in Tesco for a few months, until he got bored and decided he needed something more stimulating and became a postman, only he couldn't manage to get up early enough in the morning and I think he probably got the sack, though Maya, who is very loyal, always said it wasn't that at all. It was because his feet hurt.

In between working at proper jobs Uncle Kev has

these brilliant ideas for inventing things. He then has to try and find people who will give him some money to start actually making the things he has invented so that he can become immensely rich and Auntie Megs will be able to stop cleaning houses for people that are already immensely rich, such as Jake's mum and dad.

At the moment Uncle Kev was off on a world tour. It was his latest brilliant idea. He was going to see how far he could get by just walking and hitchhiking, starting with Europe, and then he was going to write a book about his adventures and sell it on Amazon so that Auntie Megs could stop cleaning houses, etc.

He had set off at the end of August and we were now halfway through September and Auntie Megs and Maya were still waiting to hear from him. He had warned them he wouldn't be using his mobile phone except in emergencies cos he wanted to prove that life without "all this modern technology" was still possible. Typical Uncle Kev!

At least, as Mum said, no news was good news, but I did feel a bit sorry for Maya. I could understand why she was so anxious. I would be anxious if my dad suddenly took off and we didn't know where he was or when he was coming back. Maybe I *had* been too hard on her.

"P'raps after tea," I said, "I might go round and check she's OK?"

"That would be a nice thing to do," said Mum. "Auntie Megs would appreciate that."

I said, "Yes, and we can decide what time we're leaving in the morning... We've got to go by *bus* from now on. Auntie Megs says her nerves won't stand us cycling any more."

Mum laughed. "Well, that's all right. Going by bus won't hurt you."

She didn't suggest that *I* could still cycle. It was kind of taken for granted that I'd always be there to watch over Maya. I suppose on the whole I didn't really mind. Except just sometimes I could get a bit impatient, like when I went round after tea and found her still all frail and suffering on the sofa with a great chunk of cake in her hand. Obviously nothing wrong with her appetite!

"Talk about playing it up," I said.

She looked at me reproachfully with these enormous blue eyes that she has. Big wide-apart eyes in a tiny heart-shaped face.

"It really hurt," she said. The tears were already welling up. I am convinced that Maya can actually make herself cry just by thinking about it. "If Jake hadn't been there I don't know what I'd have done."

I was about to say she'd have got up and got back on her bike, but at that moment Auntie Megs came through from the kitchen. She must have heard Jake's name cos she said, "That is such a lovely young man! Most of them wouldn't have bothered."

I thought, that was because there wasn't anything to bother *about*. But it wouldn't have been polite to say so.

"I'll see you tomorrow," I said. "Eight o'clock at the bus stop?"

Maya nodded, dreamily. "Unless Jake comes by and gives us a lift."

"Why would he do that?"

"Well… you know! If he happened to be passing," said Maya.

I looked at her, suspiciously. She had this slightly glazed and goofy expression on her face. I knew exactly what it meant.

"You've gone and done it again," I hissed, "haven't you?"

She gazed up at me, all innocence. "What?"

"Got *one of your things*." I mouthed it at her. I couldn't say it out loud, cos of Auntie Megs being there, though sometimes I think Auntie Megs only hears what she wants to hear.

"If Jake did offer you a lift," she said, "it would be extremely kind of him, but I don't think you ought to expect it. Only if he offers."

"That's all I meant," said Maya. "If he offers." And

she gave me this impish smile, like we were in some kind of conspiracy.

I shook my head. If Maya was about to embark on yet another of her all-consuming crushes life was going to be *extremely tiresome*.

CHAPTER TWO

Eight o'clock next morning found us at the bus stop, glumly waiting for a bus to appear. Well, I was glum. I hate waiting for buses! I suppose I am quite an impatient sort of person.

"This is all because of you," I grumbled to Maya. "If you hadn't made all that fuss..."

Maya gazed at me, sorrowfully. "I couldn't help it! You heard what Jake said… it was a really bad fall."

"Not that bad," I said. "You didn't have to be such a drama queen."

"I wasn't! It *hurt.* It still does. Look!" She held out her hand, palm up, to show me. "I might have needed stitches. It could have got *infected.*"

I said, "Oh, please! And why do you keep peering at cars like that?"

She started, guiltily. "I'm not!"

"Yes, you are. You're hoping Jake'll come by, aren't you?"

Except she obviously couldn't remember what sort of car he drove. *I* could remember. It was a Fiat! I'm quite good at recognising different makes of car. Dad and I sometimes look at car sites together on the internet, picking out ones Dad would like to drive. Dad usually goes for the big posh ones like BMW and Mercedes. I prefer the little ones cos I think they look more cosy. Like little Easter eggs on wheels. Maya's mum and dad don't actually have a car so she doesn't really know anything about them. I bet all she could remember about Jake's Fiat was that it was small and blue.

I'd obviously embarrassed her, but it didn't stop her peering.

"Know what?" I said.

"What?"

"You're being really obvious!"

She frowned, nibbling at a thumbnail. "What's that s'pposed to mean?"

"You're making it look like we're desperate! If you're not careful some nutter'll pull up and tell us to get in."

That scared her a bit. "We wouldn't have to do it!"

"They might try and make us."

"So we'd run!"

"*I'd* run," I said. "You'd probably trip over and fall flat on your face."

And this time Jake wouldn't be there to pick her up.

She bit her lip.

"It's what happens," I said, "when people get crushes they can't control."

She didn't try denying that she'd got a crush. Just as well cos I wouldn't have believed her. I could recognise the signs when I saw them. It wasn't the first crush she'd had. Not by a long chalk, as Dad would say. Back in Year Six she'd fallen in love with our class teacher, Mrs O'Malley. She'd trotted about after her like a little lost puppy, all beaming and trustful. It had gone on for weeks. Then last summer she'd got this massive crush on a boy called Anil, who worked at the minimart. The minimart was owned by his mum and dad, and Anil used to help out sometimes after school. Maya insisted that we call in there every single afternoon on the way home. It was like the highlight of her day – the moment she lived for. If Anil was there she was in heaven; on days when he wasn't she was cast into the deepest depths of despair.

Needless to say we always had to buy something, like a tube of Smarties or a KitKat or something. We couldn't just stand there gawping, though left to herself – that is, without me to hold her hand – it's what she probably would have done. She was never brave enough to actually say anything. She just felt this desperate need to be near him for a few minutes. It seemed to satisfy her, which was just as well since Anil showed absolutely no interest in her whatsoever. Hardly surprising. He must have been at least sixteen, maybe even older, and with Maya being so tiny he probably thought she was still just a little kid at primary school.

I don't know how long her obsession would have lasted, but at the start of the summer holidays new people took over the shop and Anil and his mum and dad disappeared and things went back to normal. It surprised me a bit cos I'd really thought Maya would be all broken up and weepy, but luckily Uncle Kev chose that moment to have one of his bright ideas: he and Maya and Auntie Megs were all going to go and live in a cottage on the Isle of Skye for a month. They were going to be entirely self-sufficient, like gas and electricity and stuff had never been invented, and then he was going to write a book about it. *Another* book.

Well, the book never got written and by the time they came home Maya had more or less forgotten about Anil, but it had been *really* tiresome while it lasted. I was just hoping this thing she was obviously getting about Jake wouldn't develop into a full-blown crush. I wasn't sure I could take it all over again!

She was still obsessively checking out every blue car that drove past. Big ones, small ones; just so long as they were blue. I hadn't realised there were so many of them. Blue must be a really popular colour! (I would have red if it was me.)

"That was a Toyota," I said as another one flashed past. "Toyota's no good."

From behind me came an indignant squawk: "Who says?"

I spun round. Oh, horrible! Linzi Baxter had snuck up behind us. I'd forgotten she got the bus.

"Ours is a Toyota," she said.

I said, "Yes, well, we're looking for a Fiat."

"Why?" said Linzi.

"Cos it's what Jake Harper drives." I couldn't resist adding, "He gave us a lift home yesterday."

"Really?" Her eyes narrowed. She didn't like that! I could almost hear the jealous thoughts whizzing round her brain: how come he's giving lifts to these total nobodies?

In the distance, at the top of the hill, I could see a bus coming towards us. As it drew near Maya suddenly clutched at me.

"Mattie, Mattie! Is that a Fiat?"

This time, she was right. It *was* a Fiat, and Jake was at the wheel. Maya was already dancing about on tiptoe, waving her arms in the air.

I made a grab at her. "Maya! Stop it!"

"But it's Jake!"

"I know, but this is a bus lane; he can't pull up here."

If I hadn't got hold of her she'd have gone running

off down the road, windmilling her arms in the hope of attracting his attention. I practically had to drag her on to the bus. Linzi followed as I pushed a reluctant Maya in front of me up the stairs. The minute we reached the top deck she raced to the nearest window to watch as Jake drove past. Linzi, to my *enormous* joy, plonked herself down next to me on the back seat.

"What's she up to?" she said.

"Oh!" I waved a hand. "I dunno. She thought he might give us a lift again."

Linzi regarded Maya in silence for a few seconds. Maya was standing with her nose pressed against the glass. She looked like a child wistfully gazing into a toyshop. Linzi shook her head.

"Pathetic," she said.

I bristled at that. It's hardly Maya's fault if she has a mum who is permanently anxious and a dad who is always rushing off in all directions, leaving them to cope without him. It would be enough, I should think, to make anyone pathetic.

"I don't know how you put up with her," said Linzi.

"She's my cousin," I said.

Lots of my friends wonder how I manage – on the whole! – to be patient with Maya; but they are my *friends*. Friends have the right to ask that sort of question. Plus they understand when I tell them about Mum and Auntie Megs being twins and me feeling the need to look out for Maya. Linzi Baxter was not my friend and I had no intention of explaining myself to *her*.

"Why did he give you a lift, anyway?" she said.

The cheek of it! What business was it of hers? I was still trying to think of a suitably crushing response when Maya suddenly decided to join in the conversation. She sank down into the seat in front of us and draped herself over the back, her eyes shining.

"He rescued me," she said. "I came off my bike, and he rescued me! He was *soooo* sweet. He picked me up and drove us home and then he *carried* me into the house cos I couldn't walk. If Jake hadn't been there I don't know what we'd have done. We might have had to call an ambulance! Mightn't we?"

I shrugged. I did wish Maya hadn't felt the need to tell everything to Linzi. She obviously wasn't impressed. She is not the sort of girl to be impressed. She gave Maya this long unblinking stare then said, "Yeah. Right."

Even then Maya didn't get the message. Eagerly she said, "Lots of boys wouldn't have bothered. I don't know why Jake did! Just cos he's a really nice young man, my mum says."

"You don't think p'raps he fancies you?" said Linzi.

She was being sarcastic. That anyone as cool as Jake Harper could possibly fancy a Year Eight nobody, especially one as small and skinny as Maya, obviously struck her as absurd. I guess it did me, too. To be honest, I hadn't even considered it. It was only Auntie Megs being his mum's cleaning lady that had made him stop. Cos he knew who Maya was, that was all. Nothing to do with him fancying her.

"Omigod," said Linzi, as Maya's face turned a bright happy scarlet, "she actually thinks he does!"

Maya at once protested that of course she didn't. "He just happened to be there!"

That was what she *said*; but I could tell she was seriously taken with the idea. Trust Linzi! This was going to make matters a whole lot worse. All we needed was Maya having fantasies that Jake had as much of a crush on her as she had on him.

People like Linzi are *such* a menace. And I was stuck with her all the way to school! It's not really that long a walk from where we get off the bus; it just seemed that it was, with Linzi droning on non-stop in my ear. All about boys. Boys that fancied her, boys that wanted to go out with her. Boys that she might *possibly* go out with, boys she wouldn't touch with a barge pole. Nothing but boys, boys, boys the whole length of Sheepcote Road! They are her main topic of conversation. Practically her *only* topic of conversation. If conversation it could be called, which strictly speaking it couldn't since I was hardly able to get a word in edgeways. Not that I tried very hard. Mostly I just tuned out, cos who's interested in hearing about Linzi Baxter and her boring stupid love life? Not me!

Once through the school gates, thank goodness, we parted company. In spite of being in the same class, Linzi and I don't really have much to do with each other. Nor, for that matter, do me and Maya. I have my friends, Maya has hers. She'd gone waltzing off to join a couple of them as soon as we'd got off the bus, leaving me on my own to suffer permanent brain damage from Linzi and her loudmouth wittering.

Fortunately on the way home that afternoon I was spared the earbashing on account of Linzi having to stay behind for something or other. All the same, I told Maya that in future, until Auntie Megs calmed down and we could use our bikes again, we were going to leave home fifteen minutes earlier. Maya immediately protested.

"I can't! I'll never be ready in time."

I said, "Well, you'd better be or I'll go without you."

There wasn't any reason I shouldn't go without her. It was only habit that kept us together.

"We'll need to be here by at least a quarter to eight."

"But why?" wailed Maya. "We got to school in plenty of time! What d'you want us to leave earlier for?"

"You can do what you like," I said. "I just don't want to get stuck with Linzi again."

"Oh," said Maya. Her face cleared. "Is that all?"

I said, "Yes. Why?" She didn't say anything to that, but her cheeks had gone a bright give-away pink. I knew what she'd been thinking. I can read her like a book! She'd thought I was trying to stop her cadging a lift from Jake. Like it was some jealous ploy on my part to come between them.

"Well, anyway," I said, "it's up to you. Either we go early or I'll use my bike."

Maya heaved a sigh. "Oh, all right! If I have to. But

if I'm doing something for you I think you ought to do something for me."

I was immediately suspicious. I said, "Like what?"

"I want us to join the Music Club!"

"The *Music* Club?"

Why on earth would she want to join the Music Club? She isn't in the least bit musical! Nor am I, to be honest. I once tried out for the junior choir, but Mrs Morgan said I wasn't quite ready for it. According to Mum she was just being kind. "What she really meant was, you have a voice like a screech owl!"

Well, and Maya's not much better. Worse if anything. She sings *flat*.

I reminded her of this, but she said just because she couldn't sing didn't mean she couldn't learn how to appreciate good music.

"You mean like classical?"

"Anything," said Maya.

"Classical's all they listen to," I said. "Beethoven and stuff. It's really boring! Emily Armstrong goes."

Emily is this girl in our class that is really sweet but has these totally weird tastes in practically everything. She *loves* poetry. She *adores* paintings. She *worships* Shakespeare. She goes to the *opera*. If it was Linzi you'd know she was just showing off; with Emily you know it's the real thing. She lives in a totally different world from the rest of us.

"Honestly," I said, "you'd be bored out of your mind."

"Mattie, *please*," begged Maya. "I want to learn!"

Well, I am never against learning, cos that would just be ignorant, but I didn't see why I had to do it. Why couldn't she get one of her friends to go with her? Tansy or Bella, for instance. They were her best mates! Why not ask them? Maya said cos they would get silly.

"They'd only start giggling."

I couldn't imagine anyone actually *giggling* at Beethoven. Fall asleep, more like. It was only when I allowed myself to be dragged along next day during the lunch break that I discovered what it was that would have made them giggle: Jake was there, sitting next to a girl from his class. He glanced up and smiled as he saw Maya. Well, I suppose he might have been smiling at both of us, but from the way Maya turned her usual bright pink I knew she was taking it as being especially for her.

No wonder she hadn't wanted her friends to come along! When Maya has one of her obsessions she makes it plain for all to see, and Tansy and Bella are gigglers at the best of times. I'm not above getting the occasional fit of the giggles myself, but I didn't find this a particularly gigglesome occasion. I was quite cross with Maya. I felt like I'd been cheated. Thanks to her I was going to waste the whole of my lunch break! I really don't know why I allow myself to be talked into these things. She is always managing to get round me. She has this way of smiling very sweetly and looking very fragile and pathetic, and I always, always fall for it.

As it was I had to sit through three quarters of an hour of mental torture. Actually, to be honest, that is not quite fair. Miss Hopwood is young and blonde and really pretty, plus she is new to teaching and still bursting with enthusiasm, so it wasn't as bad as if it had been Mrs Morgan, who is old and boring. I don't mean to be ageist, but sometimes old people *can* be boring, just like young people can, only if they're old you're not supposed to say so.

To be fair the first ten minutes were quite interesting. Miss Hopwood told us about this piece of music, *Pictures at an Exhibition*, by someone called Mussorgsky. (I think that's how it's spelt.) She said it was about two men walking round a gallery looking at paintings, and she played twiddly bits on the piano by way of illustration. Like "This is them walking round" and "This is a painting called *Ballet of the Unhatched Chicks*". Cool! I didn't mind that. But then she put on a CD and she said we all had to concentrate and see if we could recognise the bits she'd played, only I couldn't, except maybe where they were walking around. The rest was just plinking and plonking on the piano. No real tune at all.

Everybody else seemed to get it. Jake was listening really hard, you could tell, and the girl next to him looked like she was in some kind of ecstasy. Lots of people had their eyes closed. Emily not only had her eyes closed but this radiant smile on her lips. How come they all got it and not me? It made me feel I was missing something.

I stole a glance at Maya. *She* hadn't got it! She was peering in a lovelorn fashion at Jake from under her lashes, trying to make like she was lost in the music, but only managing to look faintly ridiculous. All daft and soppy. Tansy and Bella would have giggled themselves inside out. I prodded at her, but she swatted me away, angrily.

In the end I started peering at Jake, as well. I had to do *something* to keep myself awake. He is what my mum would call "tall dark and handsome". Definitely crush material, if you are the sort of person that indulges in crushes, but for goodness' sake he was eighteen! Practically grown up. And the girl sitting next to him, Hope Kennedy, was really beautiful. Thick honey-coloured hair in a ponytail, with these long, long legs like a dancer's that seemed to go on for ever. *And* she was in his year. *And* they obviously had the same taste in music.

I stole another glance at Maya. I was beginning to have bad feelings. I did so hope she came to her senses! Maddening though she could be, I would really hate for her to get hurt.

CHAPTER THREE

Well! At least I'd solved the problem of how to get us to school in the morning without Maya dramatically teetering about on the edge of the pavement, peering into cars and waving her arms every time anything small and blue appeared on the horizon. Unfortunately it hadn't solved the problem of getting back. First off she wanted to wander round the school car park, checking on the cars to see whether Jake was still there or whether he'd already left; and then when she discovered he hadn't left she purposely dawdled all the way down Sheepcote Road to the bus stop, hoping he would come by and see us waiting there.

I lectured her about it, but there is nothing you can do when someone is in the grip of an obsession. Water off a duck's back, as my dad would say. I'm not sure she even really listened. Or if she did she didn't actually *hear*.

"I'll tell you one thing," I said as we finally got on the bus, "you're not dragging me along to that music thing again."

She turned, all innocent, her eyes wide with disbelief. "Didn't you enjoy it?"

I immediately retorted, "Don't pretend that you did! You just enjoyed staring at Jake."

Pinkly, she protested, "It wasn't anything to do with Jake! I didn't even know he was going to be there."

Oh, no? What did she think, I was stupid or something?

"Honestly," said Maya, "it was the lovely music. I found it so interesting."

"Go on, then," I said. "Sing me some!"

Needless to say, she couldn't. She said that she was still learning and that was why she wanted to become a member, so that she could go along every week and hear something new.

"You know you're wasting your time," I said.

She crinkled her nose. "How d'you mean?"

"Going all soppy over him when he's sitting there with Hope Kennedy."

"But they're in the same class."

I said, "I know they're in the same class! And they like the same music, and she's absolutely gorgeous!"

I knew I was being a bit mean, rubbing it in like that, but I was still feeling sore about the way she'd tricked me. Plus it was entirely for her own good. My mum is always saying that things are "for your own good" and it is extremely annoying; but just because it's annoying doesn't make it any less true. When Maya gets one of her crushes they take over her entire life.

She sat there beside me, fiddling with the strap of her school bag. Her face had gone all puckered, so that I immediately felt – as I so often do with Maya – that I had been too harsh. Whatever a person might think of someone else's daydreams it is not very kind to trample on them.

"I'm just saying," I muttered.

"Whatever."

Maya turned, deliberately scrunching herself up against the window with her back towards me. Omigod, she was looking for Fiats again! I might just as well not have bothered.

Next day at school, during first break, I walked round the playing field as usual with a bunch of my friends. Lucy and Nasreen were ahead, earnestly discussing the possibility of Miss Cowell forgetting we were supposed to have a maths test that afternoon, since neither of them had understood a word of what she'd been talking about in our last class. Cate and I, who aren't too bad at maths, ambled along behind in the sunshine.

"So what happened yesterday?" said Cate. "With the music thing?"

I pulled a face.

"Could have told you," said Cate. "Dunno why you ever went in the first place."

"It was Maya," I said. "She told me she wanted to learn about classical music."

"*Maya?*"

"She conned me. All she wanted to do was sit and gawp at Jake Harper."

"Oh, God, she's not getting one of her things?" said Cate.

Cate knows all about Maya and her obsessions. She and I have been friends ever since primary school. I told her about Maya falling off her bike and Jake picking her up and carrying her, and she nodded, wisely.

"That'd be more than enough to set her off."

"She gets so worked up," I said. "She loses all control! It's not like when you fall for a pop star, or something. When you know it's just make-believe. You know it can't ever actually come true. Maya really believes that it *can*. Like when she got that huge crush on Anil? She honestly thought she was in with a chance. And now she thinks the same with Jake! I just know she's convinced herself he fancies her."

"Hm." Cate thought about it. "I suppose it's always possible."

"You're joking!" I said. "He's *eighteen*."

"So?"

"So she's only twelve!" And would easily have passed for just ten.

"Some guys like girls that are younger," said Cate.

I looked at her, doubtfully.

"Well, they do! How often d'you hear of old men going out with young girls?"

"Jake's not an old man," I muttered. "And why would he fancy Maya when he could have his pick?"

"Cos she's pretty?" said Cate.

"So's Hope Kennedy."

"Yeah, but she's already got someone."

I said, "Really?" And then, "How d'you know?"

"My sister's one of her best friends."

"What, and she told you?"

"No, I heard her on the phone. I wasn't eavesdropping! It's like she just has this really shrieky voice. You can hear her all over the house."

"Hm." I frowned. Could it really be that Jake fancied Maya? She *is* quite pretty, well, very pretty, actually, in a totally different way from Hope Kennedy. Hope looks like she could run the London Marathon, or go whizzing up the side of Mount Everest. Maya looks more like a puff of wind could blow her over. But Jake and Hope were an obvious couple! Jake and Maya – no...?

"Could be a budding romance," said Cate.

"What could?" Lucy had suddenly spun round, ears flapping. "Are you talking about Jake Harper?"

I couldn't very well tell her to mind her own business. She is, after all, one of my oldest friends.

"Mmmm... Jake Harper!" Nasreen clasped her hands to her bosom. What there is of it. "I could go for Jake Harper!"

"We could all go for Jake Harper," said Cate.

"But we don't," I said, "cos it would be foolish."

"Foolish is fun," said Lucy.

Fortunately at that moment the bell rang and we had to head off to class, to Miss Cowell's maths test. By the time it was over Lucy and Nasreen were so busy wailing about not having managed to answer more than half the questions that the subject of Jake Harper was forgotten. I was glad about that. I thought the fewer people who knew about Maya's latest crush the better, cos once word got out they would be bound to tease her about it and that would only make things worse. She would love it! Having her name coupled with Jake's would just fan the flames. All I could hope was that the obsession might die down as quickly as it had started up. Like if she heard from her dad, or better still if he suddenly came back home, maybe that might cure her. Maybe.

Next day was Saturday, when it was Maya's job to take Poppy for her walk. Poppy is a miniature poodle, really cute, with pretty apricot fur – well, wool I think it is. Maya and Auntie Megs are allergic to ordinary dog hair but are OK with poodles cos they don't shed. They had got Poppy when Maya and me were two years old, so she was ten by now, which is not terribly young, so we usually just took her down the hill to Layhams Park, where she could meet up with other dogs and have a bit of a play. I only went cos a) Mum said the exercise would be good for me and b) I do quite like dogs. I wouldn't actually mind having one myself if only Mum and Dad weren't both out all day at work, which Mum says wouldn't be fair on an animal.

That Saturday, instead of automatically turning left towards the park, Maya determinedly set off in the opposite direction.

I said, "Hey! Where are we going?"

"Up the hill," said Maya.

"Why? Why aren't we going to the park?"

"Cos Poppy needs some road walking. Her nails are too long! She needs to wear them down."

"Oh?" I couldn't see anything wrong with her nails. They weren't clicking and clacking on the pavement.

"Mum said," said Maya. "She said she needs roadwork."

I said, "Oh! OK."

I couldn't very well argue with Auntie Megs. All unsuspecting, I fell into step beside Maya.

"So where shall we go?"

"We'll just walk," said Maya.

We reached the top of the hill and crossed over into Baynes Road. By that time we were deep in conversation so I didn't really pay much attention to where we were headed. It wasn't until about twenty minutes later that I suddenly came to.

"Hey! This is Fitzjames Avenue," I said.

"Is it?" Maya stared round in apparent amazement,

like, *how on earth did we get here?* Like she hadn't led us there deliberately! Fitzjames Avenue was where Jake lived. It was full of big posh houses with in-and-out drives and two-car garages. Jake's house was number fifteen, right down at the far end, which Maya was perfectly well aware of cos of having been there with her mum. *This was no accident.*

"I was just following Poppy," said Maya. "I don't know why she came this way!"

Neither did I, considering Poppy had never been there before. Auntie Megs didn't take *her* when she did her cleaning.

"It's time we went back, anyway," I said.

"We can't yet," objected Maya. "She has to be out at least an hour. This is her exercise!"

"But if we walk all the way down Fitzjames," I said, "there's nowhere to go at the end of it. Just the main road."

"So we'll walk to the end and then we'll walk back."

I looked at her through narrowed eyes. "We're not going to go and hang around outside Jake's house."

Maya said, "No, but he could be in the front garden, washing his car, and we could just say hello and he might offer us a lift home!"

"Why would he do that?" I said.

"Cos his mum told Mum that if ever we needed a lift anywhere and Jake was free he'd be happy to take us. Cos of Dad being away," said Maya.

"But we don't *need* a lift."

"We will by the time we've got to the end of Fitzjames," said Maya. "Poor Poppy! She'll be tired by then."

"Excuse me," I said. "You just told me she needed the exercise."

"An *hour*," said Maya. "She's not a baby any more."

"So let's turn back right now," I said.

But she wouldn't. For such a delicate little flower (which is what Mum once yuckily called her) Maya can be infuriatingly stubborn. And totally nonsensical! But once she is in the grip of one of her obsessions there is simply no getting through to her.

"You can go back if you want," she said. "Me and Poppy'll carry on for a bit."

I was tempted. I had these visions of me and Maya standing at the gate of Jake's house, with Maya looking all pathetic and forlorn, and me bright red with embarrassment at her side. It would be just too shaming! But then, as I turned to go, I had other visions. Visions of Maya still waiting there an hour later and Auntie Megs calling Mum in a panic to know if I was back yet and if Maya was with me, and Mum saying, "Mattie, how could you? Just going off and leaving her!" Like I always had to be the responsible one.

"It's all right, you can go," said Maya.

She actually wanted me to! It immediately made me suspicious.

"I'll come," I said, "but as soon as we reach the main road we're turning round and coming *straight back*."

"Well, but of course," said Maya.

"We're not going to hang around waiting for Jake to appear."

"Of course we're not."

Of course we weren't! Like the idea had never entered her head.

"Even if he does happen to be there," I said, "you know what your mum told you? You can't expect him to *keep* giving you lifts."

"I don't," said Maya. "I wouldn't! But if he's actually *there*—"

"No!" My voice came out in a strangulated squawk. "I don't care! You actually ask him and I'll – I'll –" I spluttered – "I'll never do anything for you ever again!"

"Well, I won't if you don't want me to," said Maya. "But honestly, he wouldn't mind."

I said, "How do you know?"

"I just do," said Maya.

"*How?*"

She didn't say anything to that; just gave this little secretive smile. I frowned.

"I'm not sure this is such a good idea," I said.

"We're only walking past his house," said Maya. "There isn't any law against walking past a person's house. And anyway," she added, trying to make like she didn't care one way or another, "he probably won't be there."

As it happened, thank goodness, he wasn't. I breathed a sigh of relief.

"Please, now," I said, "can we just go back?"

For a minute I honestly thought she was going to suggest knocking at the door. But in the end, with a sigh, she let me turn her round and set off for home. I couldn't help wondering, if I'd gone off and left her there, whether she would have been bold enough to actually do it? She would never have been bold enough with Anil, but Anil had never given her any encouragement. *He* had never picked her up and carried her indoors. Really I was beginning to think that Jake should have had a bit more sense. All very well Auntie Megs saying what a lovely young man he was, but anyone could have seen it was asking for trouble – well, anyone that knew Maya. Which Jake did.

"At least," I said as we walked back down the hill, "Poppy won't need any more roadwork. I should think by now her nails must be worn practically *flat*."

CHAPTER FOUR

Sunday morning, as usual, I called round for Maya. We always take Poppy for another walk on a Sunday. It was Auntie Megs who came to the door. She seemed surprised to see me.

"Mattie!" she said. "Maya's already left."

I said, "Oh?"

"About half an hour ago. She told me…" Auntie Megs faltered. "She told me you couldn't come. She said you were busy."

"Dunno how she got that idea," I said.

"Maybe if you walk down to the park you'll bump into her."

"If that's where she's gone," I said.

A frown crinkled Auntie Megs' forehead. "Where else would she go?"

"Maybe up the hill?" I said.

"Why would she do that?" Already Auntie Megs was starting to sound concerned. We always went to the park! I couldn't very well explain that Maya was in the grip of one of her obsessions. Auntie Megs didn't know about Maya and her obsessions. Even Maya had the sense to realise they were best kept secret from her mum.

"Why would she want to walk up the hill? What's wrong with the park? Has something happened?"

As soothingly as I could I said, "No, it's just Poppy's nails."

"Poppy's nails?" Auntie Megs sounded confused.

"She said you told her to take her round the roads and wear them down a bit."

"*I* did?"

"That's what she said."

There was a pause. Auntie Megs bit her lip. "I don't remember!"

Too late, I realised… Auntie Megs hadn't said anything about Poppy's nails. There wasn't anything wrong with Poppy's nails! Maya had made the whole thing up. Now her mum was in a state thinking her memory was failing. Maya *knows* Auntie Megs gets upset. What did she think was going to happen when I called round and she wasn't there?

"Don't worry," I said. "It's probably just Maya getting in a muddle. Like thinking I was busy." I could see doubt creeping into Auntie Megs' eyes. "See, I *am* busy," I said, inventing as fast as I could. "But that's this afternoon. That's when I'm busy. Cos I'm – I'm doing things! And prob'ly *she* thought Poppy's nails looked long and – and it was me getting in a muddle and thinking she said you. So that's why we walked up the hill. Yesterday. Cos she'd noticed."

Auntie Megs twisted a strand of hair round her fingers. She has the same hair as Maya: golden brown, very straight and fine.

"So where do you think she'll have gone?"

I knew where she'd gone. Fitzjames Avenue was where she'd gone! But I didn't want to throw Auntie Megs into one of her panics.

"It all depends," I said. "Yesterday we just kind of wandered around. I'll go and have a look! See if I can find her."

I didn't bother checking out the park: I knew she wouldn't be there. Sure enough, I'd only walked a short way up the hill when I saw a little blue car approaching. I turned back and stood waiting for it as it pulled in on the corner of Maya's road. Maya, beaming happily, scrambled out with Poppy. She leaned in, through the passenger window.

"Thank you so much for the lift! Poor Poppy was so tired."

"No problem." Jake raised a hand. "Hi, Mattie!"

We both stood watching as he took off, down the hill.

"He just happened to be there," said Maya. Totally unapologetic. Absolutely *no* sense of shame. "He was coming this way anyhow."

I ignored that.

"Why did you tell your mum I was busy?" I said.

"I didn't!"

"She said you did."

"Oh. Well! She obviously didn't understand properly."

"So why didn't you wait for me?"

She couldn't think of anything to say to that. I could see her desperately trying to dredge up some kind of excuse.

"You just wanted to sneak off by yourself and see if you could cadge a lift!"

"I didn't *cadge*. He offered!"

I said, "Yeah, yeah, yeah."

"He did," insisted Maya. "He saw me and he asked if I wanted a lift. And what's it to you, anyway?"

"I just don't like to see you making an idiot of yourself."

"You're the one that's making an idiot of herself," said Maya. "I suppose you're jealous."

"*Jealous? Me?*" I was flobbergasted. Flobber, flabber. Whatever the word is. She had some nerve! "What's there to be jealous of?"

Maya gave one of her little secret smiles. Very irritating. I said, "*Well?*"

Maya said, "Well…"

"Well *what?*"

She shrugged.

"*Well what?*" I yelled it at her. Maya made a flinching movement, like I was about to hit her.

"You are just so stupid at times," I said. "And so mean to your mum!"

That shook her a bit. Indignantly she said, "How am I mean to Mum?"

"Getting her all worked up and worried in case she's losing her mind."

Maya's face puckered slightly. "What are you talking about?"

"She couldn't remember telling you that Poppy needed roadwork," I said.

Maya bit her lip. She's usually quite protective of her mum — just like I'm usually protective of her. But not today! Today I was just too angry. Her accusing me of being jealous was the last straw. What did I have to be jealous of?

"I'm going home," I said, and I turned and stalked off, down the hill.

"Mattie!" Maya's voice came wailing after me. "Mattie, I'm sorry! We could still take Poppy to the park."

"Don't want to," I said. "Not interested."

"Mattie, please…" Her feet pattered up behind me. She caught at my arm, but I wrenched it away.

"Leave me alone! I don't want to know."

I hurtled on down the hill, leaving Maya standing

forlornly with Poppy. I hardly ever get mad with her. Not properly mad. But she really can try my patience!

When I got home Dad wanted to know why I was in such a bad mood, banging doors and wearing what he calls my gargoyle face. I didn't tell him it was because of Maya. Dad's not as understanding as Mum. Mum would have discussed it with me and calmed me down, but Dad would just have started on again about Uncle Kev and how Maya and Auntie Megs were his responsibility, not mine or Mum's, and that would have made me even more cross and resentful than I was already.

By the time we met up for school next morning I'd managed to cool off a bit. I really hate it when we fall out! It doesn't happen very often, cos Maya hates it, too. One or other of us always ends up being all grovelling and apologetic. Sometimes both of us. Like that morning at the bus stop.

"I'm really sorry I accused you of being jealous," said Maya.

I said, "I should hope so! Cos I absolutely am *not*." And then, feeling generous, I added that I was sorry, too – except that I couldn't quite think what I was supposed to be sorry for. Maya quickly reminded me.

"It was really mean of you to say I'm making an idiot of myself! Jake told me, he's *always* happy to give me a lift."

I made a sort of grunting sound. I wasn't going to quarrel with her again, but just because Auntie Megs was his mum's cleaning lady and Jake was naturally kind and polite didn't mean he necessarily wanted Maya popping up every five minutes and trying to get into his car. Well, I hoped it didn't – *and not because I was jealous.* Just that Auntie Megs would be horrified if she thought there was any sort of boy/girl stuff going on. Even Mum, who is very relaxed about almost everything, wouldn't want me going out with an eighteen-year-old.

"P'raps you just ought to be a bit careful," I said.

Maya looked at me, wide-eyed. "Careful of what?"

I said, "Well... you know! Being too pushy. Some

people might even say you were throwing yourself at him."

That made her colour up.

She said, "That is so not true!"

"It so is!"

"It so is not!"

We were on the verge of falling out again. Sullenly, Maya said, "What's your problem, anyway?"

"I just don't want to see you get hurt."

"Why would I get hurt?" said Maya "What d'you think's going to happen?"

Crushingly I said, "He'll get sick of you, that's what!"

She was a bit subdued after that. We hadn't exactly quarrelled, but I knew she wasn't happy with me, and when Mum told me and Dad, later on, that there still wasn't any news from Uncle Kev, I couldn't help feeling sorry for her all over again. How scary would it be not knowing where your dad was or when – if ever – he was going to come back? I should have been more understanding. Having a slanging match really didn't help.

"To be honest," said Mum, "it's getting a bit worrying. He still hasn't been in touch. If it goes on much longer Megs is really going to crack up."

Dad, very scathingly, said, "The man is a menace. She'd be better off without him."

"Unfortunately she loves him," said Mum.

I said, "So does Maya! We had to write essays last term about our family, and Maya's was all about Uncle Kev and how wonderful he was."

Dad snorted. Mum said, "Well, of course to her he's wonderful! He's her dad."

"When he's there," said Dad.

Mum asked me, when we were alone together, how I thought Maya was coping. I said, "OK, I guess." I didn't tell her that she was totally preoccupied with getting Jake to take notice of her. I was beginning to wonder if this was what always happened when Uncle Kev went off on one of his jaunts. I seemed to recall he'd been away when she'd developed her huge great crush on Anil.

"I just hope to heaven he comes back soon," said Mum, "or at any rate gets in touch. This is where I really wish your gran were still with us! She was always so good at keeping Megs on an even keel. We do our best, don't we?" She gave me a hopeful smile. "I know it puts a lot on your shoulders and I know it makes your dad angry, but Megs is like a part of me. I can't just wash my hands of her. And never think I don't appreciate it, the way you look out for Maya. I feel bad that you have to do it, but—"

"Mum," I said, "it's OK! You don't have to feel bad. I do it cos I want to, not cos I have to."

"Oh, Mats!" Mum held out her arms. "Come and give me a hug… Maya doesn't know how lucky she is to have a cousin like you!"

I get all squishy when Mum says nice things to me. I'm more used to being told I'm too noisy, too talkative, too fidgety. I can cope far better with that!

I was especially patient with Maya for the rest of the week, but when she begged me to go with her again to the Music Club I dug my heels in. Enough was enough! If she wanted to go and gaze at Jake she would have to do it by herself.

"I don't know what you need me for anyway," I said.

"Cos otherwise I'll be on my own! There isn't anyone else from our year."

"Excuse me?" I said. "Since when has Emily not been in our year?"

Maya said Emily didn't count. "She's on another planet."

Where did Maya think *she* was?

I said, "The thing about Emily, she goes for the music."

"So do I," insisted Maya. "I'm trying to *learn*."

I told her – not being nasty, just being firm – that she would have to learn by herself. I had other things to do.

"You're right," said Cate as we wandered round the field after lunch. "It's time she stood on her own feet. I know your mums are twins and all that, but you're not always going to be there for her."

"And anyway," said Lucy, "what's she expect you to do? Act as some sort of go-between? *Please, Jake, my cousin has this gi-normous crush on you. I hope you don't mind if she stares a little bit?*"

Nasreen giggled. I supposed by now most people must have noticed that Maya was in a state of complete infatuation. Except maybe Jake himself. Boys aren't always very quick at picking up on these things.

I couldn't resist asking Maya, as we walked down Sheepcote Road after school, whether she had actually learnt anything from going to the Music Club.

"Loads!" she said.

"Like what?"

"Like…" She pressed the tip of her finger against her nose, making it go all tip-tilted. "It's difficult to explain. You're *so* not musical!"

I said, "Neither are you."

She turned her big blue eyes on me. "That's why I'm trying to learn!"

"So what was the music?"

She had to think about that. "Something called… Nigma?"

"*Nigma?*"

"It had a bulldog in it!" She announced the fact, triumphantly. "He jumped into the water and you could hear all the splashing sounds."

"And his name was Nigma?"

"Something like that." She waved a hand, impatiently. "What's it matter what it was called? It's what it *sounded* like that's important."

"I suppose *he* was there?" I said.

She nodded, pinkly. She didn't bother asking who I meant. "He's incredibly musical," she said. "He stayed behind afterwards to ask questions."

"What about Hope? Did she go?"

"Hm." Maya nodded again; not quite so enthusiastically this time. "D'you really think she's pretty?"

"Drop-dead gorgeous," I said.

"Really?" I could see Maya struggling. "I suppose her hair's not bad."

I said, "I would die for hair like that!" Long and thick and straight, like she'd laid it out on the ironing board and ironed it. And honey-blonde! I am a sort of reddish brown, very wild and wiry. Unfortunately I take after Dad in that respect. Maya takes after Mum and Auntie Megs. Although her hair is rather fine and wispy it is quite a pretty colour.

"I suppose –" Maya said it grudgingly – "some people might think she was attractive. If they like big women. She's awfully masculine."

So not true!

"*Athletic*," I said. "Like Jake."

I wasn't quite sure why I'd said that. I knew it would upset her, but she needed to face up to things. Jake is athletic; Hope is athletic. Maya is anything but! We had reached the bus stop by now and were standing there, waiting for our bus, when a car drove past. It was Jake's Fiat. There was someone with him. I couldn't see who it was; just caught a glimpse of blonde hair. Maya had obviously caught it, too.

Jealously she said, "That wasn't her, was it?"

"Dunno," I said. "Might have been."

"*Honestly?*"

"It certainly looked like her," I said.

"I'm not sure that it was," said Maya.

"Well, whoever it was," I said, "she had gorgeous blonde hair."

I suppose I could have set her mind at rest by telling her I knew for a fact that Jake and Hope Kennedy weren't an item, so even if it had been her it didn't mean anything. But that would have been encouraging her, and encouraging her was the last thing I wanted to do.

"I think you have to accept," I said kindly, "that you're not the only person Jake takes in his car. He does give lifts to people other than you."

CHAPTER FIVE

That Saturday we had a really good walk. Maya had promised me, *on her honour*, that a) she would wait for me and b) we would take Poppy to the park as usual.

"Cos her nails are nice and short now. And I know you don't want us doing any more roadwork."

She made it sound as if we were going to the park

as a special favour to me. I automatically felt suspicious. There was an air of secret excitement about Maya, like something was going on that she didn't want me to know about. Plus I found it hard to believe that she'd given in so easily.

It was possible she had just run out of excuses, but experience had taught me that Maya in the grip of an obsession could be really sneaky.

When we got to the park that Saturday I half expected Jake's Fiat to pull up at the kerb. Or even to see Jake himself, in the park. I just couldn't understand why Maya was all quietly fizzing and bubbling. What had she got planned?

We let Poppy off the lead and walked slowly after her, round the path, as she went joyfully skipping off across the grass to greet her friends.

"This is so much nicer for her than roads," I said.

Maya agreed that it was, now that her nails were short. Still keeping up the pretence even though she *knew* I was on to her.

"By the way," I said, "That music with the bulldog…"

"Nigma."

"*Enigma*. Variations."

She looked at me wonderingly, like, *what is she talking about?*

"Emily told me. She said it's *Enigma Variations* and it's by someone called Elgar. She says her dad has it on CD and she's been listening to it since she was five years old."

"*Yuck*," said Maya.

"She wasn't boasting," I said. Emily doesn't boast. She just takes that sort of thing for granted, like it's perfectly normal. It obviously is, in her family. "I told her you were trying to learn about classical music, and she said if you wanted you could borrow her dad's CD."

"We haven't got a CD player," said Maya.

I said, "We have."

"Hm." She didn't sound madly enthusiastic. "I s'ppose I could give it a go."

"If you listened to it over and over," I said, "some of it might kind of sink in, then you could sing it to Jake next time you manage to talk him into giving you a lift. That would impress him!"

I only said it to be provocative. Maybe to make her a bit ashamed of herself. She wasn't supposed to take it seriously! But omigod, I could tell that she was. She was actually considering it.

"So could I borrow your CD player, do you think?"

"Well, you could," I said, "though prob'ly best not, now I come to think about it. Considering you can't sing in tune."

"Neither can you," said Maya.

"What's that got to do with it? I'm not the one that wants to impress her boyfriend! Not that he *is*," I said hastily. Not quite quick enough! A happy pink glow of contentment was already spreading over her face. I really don't know why I say these things; it's just putting ideas in her head. A sort of mischief gets into me and I can't resist it.

"He's far too old," I said, "and in any case he's probably already got a girlfriend."

The pink glow slowly faded. "You don't really think he's going out with Hope Kennedy?"

"Well, he was giving her a lift," I said.

"If it *was* her," said Maya.

"Whoever it was."

"Doesn't mean it was his girlfriend!"

"I put it to you…" I said. It's what Dad says to Mum when he wants to make a point: "I put it to you". "How likely is it that someone like Jake Harper wouldn't have a girlfriend?"

Maya munched uncertainly on her lower lip.

"Well, there you go," I said. "I rest my case." Another of Dad's favourite expressions, meaning *end of*. It drives Mum mad! Maya just fell silent. She didn't seem to be sulking; just preoccupied. I tried to think of some way of changing the subject. I really didn't want to talk about Jake.

"You know your mum is coming round this afternoon,"

I said. "Mum's going to do her hair for her. Are you coming as well?"

"I can't this afternoon," said Maya. "I've got things to do."

"Like what?" I said.

"Just things," said Maya.

We don't usually keep secrets from each other, but she obviously didn't intend to tell me. Something was up, and I didn't know what! It wasn't long before I found out. I was sitting in the kitchen while Mum saw to Auntie Megs' hair. I like to watch Mum at work. Sometimes in the holidays I go and help out at her salon, just sweeping the floor or making cups of coffee for the customers. I might want to be a hair stylist when I grow up; I'm not sure. I might also want to be an animal trainer. I haven't yet decided. It seems to me that if you take up hairdressing you have to be prepared to do a lot of *talking*. It is not just about cutting and styling, you have to keep up this chitchat all the time. (Chitchat is what Dad calls it.) I do, quite naturally, talk a fair bit, but I am not sure I would want to do it as part of my job. Mum is really good at it. Like today, while she was busy blow-drying she was also doing her best to reassure Auntie Megs that nothing had happened to Uncle Kev and that she was bound to hear from him soon.

"You know what he's like! Time gets away from him. He'll come breezing back home and you'll say, *Where have you been all these weeks?* And he'll be, like, *Weeks? I don't believe it!* Look what happened when you got married... ten minutes late for his own wedding!"

Auntie Megs gave a rather tearful sort of smile. "I thought he wasn't going to turn up."

"But he did! He always does – in the end. He just has no sense of—" Mum broke off. "Did I hear someone at the door?"

I leapt up. "I'll go!"

"Was that the bell?" shouted Dad, from somewhere upstairs.

"It's all right," I yelled. "I've got it!"

Just as well it was me that answered the door and not Dad. He would have been at a total loss! I was a bit at a loss myself. I found Maya standing in the porch, tears streaming down her face and her head all done up in a towel.

I said, "What's the matter? What's wrong?"

She couldn't speak for sobbing. I dragged her in and pulled her through to the kitchen.

"Maya!" cried Auntie Megs. "What's happened?"

"I –" Maya choked. "I – I – my hair!"

This last bit came out in a loud wail. Mum put down the dryer.

"All right," she said. Very calm – Mum is always calm. "Let me see. What have you done?"

Gently but firmly Mum unwound the towel. Auntie Megs gave a shriek. I nearly shrieked with her. Maya's hair had turned bright yellow and looked like bits of stringy elastic.

"Oh, dear," said Mum. "What did you use?"

Maya gave a great snotty sniffle and wiped her nose

on the back of her hand. Pretty disgusting, but I forgave her. I reckoned I'd be giving snotty sniffles if I'd gone and turned my hair into bits of yellow elastic – especially when Mum reached out and gave a little experimental tug and some of the bits broke off.

Auntie Megs screamed. Maya sobbed. Even I felt somewhat alarmed. Only Mum refused to panic.

"Maya," she said, "tell me what you used."

Maya gulped, and choked. "It was something – something I got – from the chemist. I just put it on – like it said – and left it for a bit, and…"

"How long?" said Mum.

"I don't know! Not very long."

"Obviously longer than you should. Did you not read the directions?"

"I read them," wept Maya. "I just thought – I thought…"

"You thought if you left it on longer it would be more effective. I'm afraid it's damaged your hair, but not to worry, we'll do what we can. You won't go bald! Let me just finish with your mum."

"No! No!" Auntie Megs waved a hand. "See to Maya first!"

"Well, I can't work miracles," warned Mum, "but let's see what we can manage."

Mum was wrong: she *can* work miracles! It did take a bit of time, though. To begin with she smothered Maya's hair in conditioner and wrapped her up in a plastic bath cap and a big fluffy towel and made her stay like that for half an hour. We all sat round the kitchen table to keep her company, with Mum and Auntie Megs drinking cups of tea and me and Maya nibbling biscuits, and Auntie Megs asking over and over, "What on earth made you do it?" I could have told her! She wanted to have blonde hair like Hope Kennedy. Now she'd got yellow hair, all gluggy and spongy. No wonder she'd arrived on the doorstep sobbing her heart out.

Dad looked in at one point, but quickly disappeared again. The sight of a weeping Maya and a teary-eyed Auntie Megs was obviously too much for him. Dad can't cope with emotion. He leaves all that sort of thing to Mum.

"What happens next?" I asked, when Maya had obediently sat there for half an hour.

"Next we shampoo," said Mum.

"Is it all going to fall out?" quavered Maya.

"Not all of it," said Mum, cheerfully. "Just the ends."

"What on earth made you do it?" wailed Auntie Megs, for about the tenth time.

"I thought it would look nice," sobbed Maya. The prospect of losing half her hair had brought on yet another bout of weeping.

"It will look nice," promised Mum. "Trust me!"

Mum really is a genius when it comes to hair. First she used some special kind of shampoo that she keeps in her salon for people that have gone and ruined their hair by giving themselves bad perms or by not properly following the directions on bottles of bleach; next she rinsed through with something that would hopefully – as she said – "tone things down a bit". Then lastly she took the scissors and ruthlessly snipped and snapped until all the frizzly bits were lying on the floor like shrivelled worms and Maya was sitting with her eyes squeezed shut cos she couldn't bear to watch. I don't expect I'd have been able to watch, either, if it had been me. I am not in the least bit vain, but who wants to end up bald? Especially when they're in the clutches of a huge gigantic crush on someone as cool as Jake Harper.

Maybe, I thought, it would teach Maya a lesson. I tried telling myself that it served her right. Running after a boy of eighteen who wouldn't even look twice at her! I couldn't *believe* he would look twice at her. No matter how tiny and pretty she was. Not that she would look very pretty with half her hair gone. It could actually be called a blessing in disguise, if it stopped her pursuing him. She'd hardly want to draw attention to herself without any hair!

I had reckoned without Mum and her genius.

"There!" Mum switched off the dryer and reached out for her mirror. "How about that?"

A slow beam of wonderment spread itself across Maya's face as she gazed at her new image. Mum turned, triumphantly, to me and Auntie Megs.

"So what do you think?"

"Mum," I cried, "that's brilliant!"

I was lost in awe. My mum could be a stylist to the stars! Maya's hair was no longer bilious yellow, but a soft golden brown, cut very short, almost like a little cap fitted to her head, with tiny tendrils snaking round her ears.

"This is something I've been itching to do for ages," said Mum. "I knew a shorter style would suit you! Now you look like a little elf."

Mum sounded so proud and happy that I couldn't make my usual being-sick noise. Little elf... *bluuurgh!* But Mum was right, like she always is. Maya couldn't stop admiring herself in the mirror. Even Auntie Megs was full of smiles.

"You should have done it sooner!"

"I tried," said Mum. "She'd never let me. Now! Let's

get back to you and see if we can turn you into an elf as well." She was only joking, of course. You can't have middle-aged elves! Though I know, from seeing photos, that Auntie Megs – and Mum – had both been elflike when they were young. I do sometimes wish that I could be elflike myself instead of what Miss Phillips, our PE teacher, once called sturdy.

I think I must have heaved a bit of a sigh as I looked at Maya with her new elfin cut, cos Auntie Megs immediately said, in kindly tones, "How about you, Mattie? Have you ever thought of changing your hairstyle?"

Mum laughed and said, "To what? Her hair's stuck up like a lavatory brush since the day she was born!"

It really is just as well I am not vain. Hair like a lavatory brush! I thought, *Thank you, Mum. Thank you very much!*

"Takes after her dad," said Auntie Megs. And then, because she had said the word dad, she quickly put an arm round Maya's shoulders and hugged her and said, "You take after me and your Auntie Ray, don't you?"

And then she glanced at Mum and gave a little warning frown and a shake of the head, like, *Whatever we do, we don't talk about Kevin.*

"So, all's well that ends well," said Mum, once we were alone again, "but I have to say that really is quite one of the daftest things Maya's ever done! What on earth possessed her?"

"She's got this thing about Jake," I said. "She thinks he goes for girls with blonde hair."

"Really? That's why she did it?"

"It's kind of embarrassing," I said. "Ever since he carried her home that day she came off her bike she's had this mad crush on him. She keeps expecting him to give her lifts everywhere, just cos Mrs Harper said he wouldn't mind."

"He probably doesn't," said Mum. "He's very tolerant."

"But, Mum," I said, "she takes advantage!"

"I wouldn't worry too much," said Mum. "Jake's a big boy: he can look after himself. I'm sure if he starts to get fed up he'll find some way of discouraging her."

Glumly I said, "That'd prob'ly just make her even worse. She gets, like, *obsessed*, you know?"

Mum shook her head. "She's a sad little creature. Your Auntie Megs was telling me how Maya sometimes cries herself to sleep at night, worrying whether she's ever going to see her dad again. And if she's got a bit of a crush on Jake – well! It's hardly surprising. She'd probably respond the same way to anyone who was sympathetic. It's just good that it was Jake, and not somebody who'd be unkind to her. Don't worry! He's a sensible boy, I'm sure he'll be able to handle the situation."

I must still have looked a bit doubtful, cos Mum laughed and said, "Rest assured, she won't be the first girl to have developed a crush on him! He's probably used to it by now. Try not to be too hard on her! We've all been there."

I hadn't. Was Mum saying that *she* had?

"Way back when I was your age," said Mum, "me and my best friend both got this huge crush on a Year Twelve boy. He was in the Rugby team. We thought he was wonderful! We used to follow him about, all over the school. Quite embarrassing, now I look back on it."

"What did *he* do?" I said.

"Oh, he didn't do anything! Far too grand to notice the likes of us."

But Jake *had* noticed Maya. And with her new elfin haircut he would notice her even more. Any boy would. It wasn't that I was jealous. I really wasn't! Just that I couldn't help wondering where Maya's daydreams were going to lead her.

CHAPTER SIX

Everyone at school commented on Maya's hair, saying how lovely it was. I said proudly that it was my mum who had cut it.

I didn't tell them how Maya had tried to turn herself blonde and ended up with a head full of bright yellow elastic, all bobbling up and down and breaking off like bits of twig. Maya didn't tell them, either. She actually tried to take some of the credit!

"I just felt it was time for a change. I knew it would suit me better if I had it short."

I did reckon that was a bit of a cheek. I said so, in private, to Cate. I told her everything – I couldn't help it. I just had to get it off my chest.

"If it hadn't been for Mum she'd be completely bald!"

"Might have been a good thing," said Cate. "At least it would have stopped her running after Jake. Now it's made her all madly full of herself. And even prettier!"

I said, "Hm." And then, hopefully, "Maybe Jake won't notice. Boys don't always. *Men* don't. My mum once put silver streaks in her hair, just for fun, and it was weeks before Dad suddenly asked her if she knew she was going grey."

"That's cos he's a married man," said Cate. "People stop noticing things when they've been married a while. I bet he'd have noticed soon enough when they were young."

"I dunno," I said. "Mum swears he wouldn't notice if she wore a bucket on her head. She says he's always been like that."

Cate thought about it. "That's probably just your dad," she said. "Not being rude or anything, but your dad's, like... not very *stylish*, if you know what I mean? Jake's more kind of modern."

I said, "Well, he ought to be! He's only eighteen. My dad's *forty*."

"And Maya," Cate reminded me, "is only twelve."

I was quite glad that at that moment the bell rang and we had to go back into school. I didn't want her telling me yet again that boys sometimes liked going out with girls that were younger than they were. I almost wished I'd never told her about Maya's embarrassing crush in the first place, though probably by now she'd have noticed for herself.

At the end of school we were wandering down to the main exit in a big bunch: me, Maya, Cate, Lucy, Nasreen and, for some reason, Linzi. She didn't usually attach herself, but hey, it's a free world. You can't stop people walking with you. Unfortunately.

We were almost at the gates when Jake overtook us, on his way to the car park. He was dangling his car keys from one finger. So cool! I could understand Maya having a crush on him. I didn't *blame* her having a crush on him. It's just a question of keeping things in proportion – which Maya, of course, can never do.

As he strode past, Jake glanced back over his shoulder and stuck up a thumb.

"Like the hair!"

There was a stunned silence. The great Jake Harper condescending to notice that a Year Eight nobody had had her hair restyled! Maya's face, needless to say, was lit up like a sunrise.

Cate dug her elbow into my ribs. "Told you so," she whispered.

Even Cate, at times, can be annoying. "It doesn't actually mean anything," I said. "Maya's like his little sister. He's known her since she was a baby, practically. Well, since she was five years old." Which was when Auntie Megs had started cleaning for his mum. "He's kind of, like, *protective* towards her."

"You reckon?" said Cate. "Seems to me more like he fancies her."

I said, "*Jake?*" I was quite shocked. How could she even suggest such a thing? "That's ridiculous!"

Cate shrugged. "If you say so."

She obviously wasn't convinced, which was a bit worrying since Cate is usually so calm and sensible about things. I'm the one that that's prone to exaggeration. Well, according to Mum, that is.

"Don't worry," said Cate, kindly. "I don't suppose he'd actually snog her."

Snog her?

"That is so disgusting!" I said.

"Well, exactly," said Cate. "Which is why I expect he wouldn't do it. So long as she doesn't keep throwing herself at him."

"How can I stop her?" I said. "I can't keep an eye on her all the time!"

"Course you can't. She's got to exercise a *bit* of self-control."

"Who?" said Linzi, spinning round. "Who are you talking about? Are you talking about Mr Cool?"

"As a matter of fact," said Cate, "we were having what's called a private conversation."

"Oh! Well." Linzi tossed her head. "Sorry, I'm sure. What *I* don't understand is how come *he* gets to drive to school? Cluttering up the car park! Just cos he's a prefect!"

What *was* her problem? Jealousy, no doubt. Just because he'd noticed Maya's hair.

Linzi really does get on a person's nerves. Always so *intrusive*. And of course we got stuck with her on the bus; just me and Maya. The others all live in the opposite direction. Fortunately the bus was quite full so I didn't have to sit next to her, but there was no shaking her off as we walked up the hill. She is someone who never knows when she is not welcome. Maya, needless to say, *entirely* opted out. Just dawdled along behind us with this big soppy beam on her face while Linzi drivelled on about Jake. Why couldn't he come by bus? Why couldn't he cycle?

"Imagine," she said, "if he cycled he could get all dressed up in Lycra." She gave a little snigger. "Think what that would do to her!"

We both glanced round at Maya, still trailing behind. Still with this big soppy beam on her face. She was obviously lost in some dream world of her own. Probably hadn't heard a word we'd said. So *that,* I thought triumphantly, was a wasted effort on Linzi's part. She might just as well have saved her breath.

Two seconds later Jake himself drove past us, up the hill. He tooted his horn and waved, and me and Maya both waved back.

"Well! So he didn't offer you a lift," said Linzi.

"He would have done," said Maya, "if I'd asked him."

"Didn't think you had to ask."

I thought, omigod, this is really going to set her off. I sought frantically for a way to change the subject, but couldn't immediately think of anything. Maya meanwhile, of course, couldn't just let it rest.

"I don't *have* to ask," she assured Linzi. "I'm just saying, if I *did*. But if he saw I needed one he'd always offer."

"He didn't just now," said Linzi.

"That's cos I don't need one. We're nearly home. If he'd seen me at the *bottom* of the hill…"

"What?" said Linzi. "What would he have done?"

Maya opened her mouth to reply, but I got in first.

"Can we just stop this?" I said.

"She started it," grumbled Maya.

"Doesn't mean you have to keep on. Let's just *go*." I grabbed Maya by the arm and dragged her off. "There is absolutely no point," I said, "taking the least bit of notice of anything that girl ever says."

Next day, at the end of school, we actually managed to reach the bus stop without having Linzi as an attachment.

I said, "Phew! We made it."

"Made what?" said Maya. And then, no doubt seeing a look of intense irritation spread itself over my face, "Oh! Yes. Linzi."

It was only what I'd been talking about for the past few minutes, rushing us down the road with cries of "Quick, quick, before she catches us!" Maya can really be so vacant at times. "I wouldn't mind so much," I said, "if you didn't have this habit of expecting me to cope with her by myself. But honestly, you just wander around in some kind of dream world. And now look what's happening! It's starting to rain. I knew it would! I should have brought my umbrella. We're going to get absolutely drenched!"

"Hm." Maya quite obviously hadn't been listening to a word I'd said. Again.

"*Oi.*" I poked at her. "Did you hear me? I said we're going to get d—" I stopped. "Hey!" I cried. "Where are you going?"

"I just remembered —" she flung it at me over her shoulder — "I've forgotten my maths homework!"

I watched as she raced back up the road. I had no intention of going after her. No intention of waiting for her, either. The bus was coming and so was the rain! Maya could get drenched if she wanted. I didn't see why I should.

But after all that, guess what? At the very last minute Linzi appeared, charging across the road and bulldozing her way on to the bus right behind me.

"Made it!" she said.

I gritted my teeth. It was exactly what I'd said myself just two minutes earlier when I thought we'd got away with it.

"What's Little Miss Airy Fairy doing, running back into school?"

"Forgotten her maths homework," I said.

"Or forgotten something else," said Linzi.

I eyed her with distaste. "Like what?" I said.

"Search me! I'm not her keeper."

I didn't give her the satisfaction of asking what she was talking about. I really didn't want to know. I really didn't *care*. The inner workings of Linzi Baxter's mind are of no interest to me whatsoever. At least with Maya you can be pretty sure it's just daydreams. With Linzi it could be anything.

By the time we got off the bus the rain was crashing down just like I'd known it would. Linzi said, "Ooh, you're going to get soaked!"

She had an umbrella. It was only a mini one, about the size of a mushroom. Even if we'd huddled together it wouldn't properly have protected us, but anyway she didn't offer. I wasn't bothered. I don't really mind a bit of rain, and anyway who'd want to huddle with Linzi Baxter? At least it gave me the excuse to go galloping off up the hill by myself.

I arrived home dripping and squelching and wet all over. Mum was still at work; she doesn't usually get back till about half-past five. When I was little I used to go round to Auntie Megs', but once I was at secondary school Mum said I was old enough to be trusted on my own. She says that on the whole – "on the whole" – I am quite sensible. Maya still comes to us if Auntie Megs isn't there, but that is mostly because of Auntie Megs being such a worrier.

I stripped all my clothes off and put them in the washing machine, switched on to spin, then changed into a sweatshirt and jeans and settled down to homework. It's always a temptation *not* to settle down, to leave it till after tea, or even till bedtime, or even worse till next morning, but I do believe in getting boring stuff out of the way as soon as possible. I guess this is what Mum means about me being sensible.

I finished off my maths in double quick time and sat for a minute thinking about Maya, dashing back to school. Forgetting her homework wasn't anything new: she was always forgetting it. But actually bothering to go all the way back for it? *That* was new. On the other hand Miss Cowell had been rather unpleasant just lately on the subject of people forgetting their homework. She had said if there was any more of it there would be trouble. She hadn't said what trouble, but maybe

Maya had thought it best not to find out. If, that is, she had been listening, and not dreaming about Jake or writing his name over and over in her rough book.

The telephone rang and I went to answer it. I guessed it would be Maya wailing that she'd got soaked and why hadn't I waited for her, but it turned out to be Auntie Megs in one of her states.

"Mattie!" she said. "Where's Maya?"

"Oh," I said, "isn't she home yet? She had to go back for her maths homework."

"But it's nearly half past four! Where can she have got to?"

Carefully, so as not to throw Auntie Megs into a panic, I said, "She's probably still waiting for the bus. You know how sometimes they come along in clumps and then there's nothing for ages."

"But it's pouring with rain," said Auntie Megs. "She'll get soaked!"

"Yes, I did, too," I said. "I forgot to take my umbrella."

"Maya forgot to take her phone! It's here on the

table. I really d— oh!" Auntie Megs broke off. "She's here!"

"Is she dripping wet?" I said.

"No!" Auntie Megs gave a little happy laugh. "Jake's brought her in his car."

So it hadn't been anything to do with Miss Cowell and her dire threats. It hadn't been anything to do with maths homework at all. Maths homework had just been an excuse. She had quite deliberately gone back to cadge a lift. And I had been fooled!

Maya herself rang me a bit later. Even before I could say anything she was falling over herself to get it out: "I didn't ask him!" She sounded triumphant. "I didn't have to! He saw me standing there and he said, *Oh dear, you're going to get wet. You'd better hop in and I'll give you a lift.* So I did!"

"So why did it take you so long to get home?" I said.

"Oh! Well, that was because – because – well! I stopped to talk to someone and then it started to rain and I was just on my way out when I bumped into

Jake, and he was about to get into his car and that's when he saw me and said, *Oh dear, you're going to get wet* and offered me a lift. Just like I told Linzi he would. Without me having to ask, cos I *didn't*."

"But you didn't get home till gone half past four," I said. "How long did you stop and talk?"

"Ages," said Maya.

Or she'd hung around for ages, watching Jake's car and waiting for him to appear.

"Who were you talking to?" I said.

"Just people," said Maya. She could have told me it was none of my business. The fact that she didn't showed me she felt guilty. "But anyway," she added, "we didn't drive straight home."

I said, "*Oh?*"

"Jake had to go and get petrol. And there were hold-ups. All the way."

"Well," I said, "your mum was starting to get worried. She didn't know where you were and she couldn't ring you, cos you'd gone and forgotten your phone. What's the point of having a phone if you don't take it with you?"

"Like what's the point of having an umbrella?" said Maya. "Did you get soaking wet?"

"I not only got soaking," I said, "I got caught by Linzi. *Again*."

"Oh, poor you!" said Maya. "If you'd come back to school with me, Jake could have given you a lift, as well. I was so lucky he was there! I didn't get wet hardly at all."

Maddening. Absolutely maddening!

CHAPTER SEVEN

"Guess what?" Maya came jubilantly prancing after me as we made our way back into school after lunch break the next day.

I said, "What?" She'd just come from her Music Club meeting. It was the third week in a row that she'd been. I had to admit, I was quite impressed. I knew *why* she was going, but I never would have thought she'd have that much stamina; not even for the chance of being near the beloved.

"I think Hope's given up!" She announced it with an air of beaming satisfaction. "Jake was there, but not her!"

I said, "No, I know. She was playing rounders."

"Ha!" Maya's voice was full of scorn. "Fancy choosing to play rounders when she could have been listening to beautiful music."

"She had to play," I said. "It's the inter-house rally. She's team captain."

"Oh. Well! Anyway. Whatever. Me and Jake sat next to each other." She brought it out with an air of pride, like, *What do you think of that?* "It was him who chose where to sit," she assured me. "I didn't go and sit next to *him* cos I knew you wouldn't like it if I did that. You'd say I was being pushy."

And since when did she take any notice of anything I said?

"I'm not pushy," said Maya. "I don't have to be!"

I couldn't help wondering if Jake had really gone and sat next to her, or whether, more likely, he'd arrived late and there was only the one seat left. I reckoned that was probably what had happened. Why else would he go and sit next to a lowly Year Eight, even if she was like his little sister? It wasn't what Year Twelves *did*.

"What's more to the point," I said – another of Dad's pet phrases! It's what he says when Mum is going on about something and he can't get her to stop. "What did you actually listen to?"

"Oh, it was lovely! It was people singing."

I said, "Singing what?"

"Songs. Opera. Something!" She waved a hand, impatiently. "I can't remember exactly, but Jake asked me if I'd enjoyed it and I said yes, cos I did, and then he said if I'm interested in music why didn't I try out for the choir, and—" She stopped, indignantly. "What's your problem?"

"Oh, pardon me while I try not to die laughing," I said. "Oops! Sorry, I can't help it." I clutched at my ribs. "Oh, that is so funny! You trying for the choir."

"Why shouldn't I?" said Maya.

"Cos you so can't sing!"

"I so can!"

"Just not in tune," I said.

"Well, anyway –" she said it rather sulkily – "Jake thinks it would be a good idea. And now that I'm learning about music I probably *could* get into the choir."

"Yes, and pigs might fly," I said. I know it wasn't very original, but you can't always be thinking of clever things to say, and anyway I was too gobsmacked. Jake had obviously never heard Maya sing! I did think it was a bit irresponsible of him, though, to be encouraging her. He was probably just trying to be kind and take an interest, but it would only make her all upset and disappointed when she was turned down.

"By the way," I said, as we went into school, "Mum's

asked me if I'll go and help out in the salon for a couple of hours after school on Friday cos the new girl she got is off sick. D'you want to come? It's quite fun."

"Would we get paid?" said Maya.

"Well, probably not both of us," I said, "cos Mum only needs one. But I'd share with you! You could put it towards Auntie Megs' birthday present."

Saturday morning we were going to go shopping together to buy presents for our mums. We always did it together cos of their having the same birthday.

"So d'you want to?" I said.

"No, it's all right," said Maya. "I've got enough saved up for what I want to buy."

"But you could buy her something even nicer!"

I could see that she was tempted. But obviously the thought of me going into town and leaving her on her own to cadge yet another lift from Jake was even more tempting. Cos it was what she was going to do. I just knew it!

* * *

"All on your own?" said Mum, when I turned up at *His 'n' Hers* on Friday after school. (*His 'n' Hers* is the name of Mum's salon. It's mostly only Hers that come in, but sometimes she gets a His or two. Sometimes she even gets a His that wants to be bleached or have a perm!)

"So where's Maya?" said Mum. "Not coming?"

"I asked her," I said. "But we didn't think you'd really need both of us."

"I could have used her," said Mum, "if she'd wanted. I wouldn't like her to feel left out."

"It's OK," I said. "She's quite happy hanging around the school car park hoping Jake'll give her a lift."

"Oh." Mum pulled a face. "Still in the throes, is she? Still got her crush?"

"Mum," I said, "Maya's crushes go on for ever!"

"Ah, well," said Mum, "it's always fun while it lasts. Now, let's see what we can find for you to do… Could you bear to tidy up the back room for me? With Suzanne off sick none of us has had a chance to get round to it."

Tidying up the back room wasn't as much fun as

being in the salon, but I couldn't really complain. After all, I *was* being paid for it. Mum said before I started perhaps I could just make two cups of coffee for the ladies who were under the dryer.

"The one near the window is Mrs Armitage, the other is Jake's mum."

I said, "Oh! I didn't realise Jake's mum was here."

"She comes in every Friday," said Mum. "That's black, by the way, and no sugar. The other lady would like white with two sugars. OK?"

I scuttled off, happily. I always like to feel that I'm being useful. By the time I came out, Mum was busy shampooing someone else, so I delivered the coffees myself. Mrs Harper smiled up at me.

"Thank you so much, Mattie! Greatly appreciated."

I watched, rather wistfully, as Mum finished her shampooing. I would so love it if she let me have a go! I know I wouldn't scald people, which is what she's scared of. I hoped for a moment she might ask me to stay and hand out rollers, which sometimes she does if there's nothing else that needs seeing to, but she said, "OK, Mattie? Tidy up? It's a big job out there."

I said, "OK!" Obediently I ducked behind the curtain into the back room. Mum was right! It looked like a tornado had blown through the place. Bottles and jars all spilling out their contents, dirty cups and plates in the sink, waste basket overflowing. It was a pity, I thought, that Maya hadn't wanted to come and help. It's always more fun with two of you. I wondered where she was, right now. Sitting in the car with Jake was my bet. She had *no shame* at all.

Mum must have got Mrs Harper out from under the dryer, cos I suddenly heard them talking on the other side of the curtain. I didn't listen on purpose! I didn't have to. The curtain is quite thin and both Mum and Mrs Harper have these carrying sort of voices. In any case, conversations that people have in hairdressing salons aren't really *private*, I don't think.

I heard Mum say, "I do hope Maya isn't making a nuisance of herself with Jake."

And then Mrs Harper, sounding a bit surprised: "No! Not that I've heard. Why?"

"It's just that I gather she's got a bit of a crush on him."

"Oh!" Mrs Harper laughed. "I'm sure he can deal with it."

"So long as he doesn't feel under pressure. I know he was kind enough to offer her and her mum a lift if they needed it, but Maya really seems to be taking advantage."

"I shouldn't worry too much," said Mrs Harper. "To be perfectly honest there's nothing he likes more than driving that car! He'd be in it all day long if he had his way."

"All the same," said Mum. "I wouldn't like to think she was imposing on him. Just because he was kind enough to pick her up that time she came off her bike."

"Yes, I heard about that. Her mum told me. She was so grateful! But it's what any boy would do."

"You think?" said Mum.

"Well! Maybe not. But don't forget Jake's known her

since she was tiny. I'd have been very cross with him," said Mrs Harper, "if he *hadn't* stopped to help."

"It's just unfortunate," said Mum, "it came at a time when she's especially vulnerable, what with her dad going off and not bothering to get in touch."

There then followed a load of stuff about Uncle Kev and how selfish and irresponsible he was, and how Auntie Megs shouldn't be left to cope on her own, and really it wasn't any wonder if poor little Maya was desperately insecure.

I'd heard it all a zillion times before so I kind of stopped listening for a bit, not that I'd actually *been* listening. It was more, like, taking care not to slam cupboard doors or clatter too much. Usually when I tidy stuff up I like to do it quite vigorously, which is the way I do pretty much everything. Mum sometimes complains about the noise I make.

"Don't do anything by halves, will you?" she goes, clapping her hands over her ears.

Well, but why would you? What would be the point?

I ran water very busily into the sink and set about doing this massive clear-up job on all the dirty plates and dishes that had piled up. I wondered if Mrs Harper would say anything to Jake about Maya having a crush on him. I hadn't expected Mum to tell her, though I supposed it didn't actually matter. Practically the whole of our class knew about it, so why not Mrs Harper? And even if she did tell Jake, I couldn't really see that it was a problem. It was all so obvious that he ought to have noticed it for himself by now.

I swished energetically in the sink so that Mum and Mrs Harper's voices were pretty well blotted out. I couldn't even be sure that they were still talking. And then, in between tossing knives and forks across the room and seeing if I could manage to lob them into the cutlery drawer (which mostly I couldn't), I heard Mrs Harper say, "I'm pretty certain he *does* have a girlfriend," and I immediately stopped lobbing things cos – well! She could be talking about Jake. And it couldn't be secret or she wouldn't be doing it in the middle of a hairdressing salon where just anybody could hear. I mean, if there had been anybody about, which in fact there wasn't apart from the lady under the dryer and I should think you're pretty much deaf when you're under a dryer. But *I* was there! She knew I was there, working away on the other side of the curtain. So it obviously wasn't secret and I didn't have to feel guilty. I just went on doing my job, but doing it *quietly*, the way Mum likes, so as not to be intrusive. That's all.

"The thing is," said Mrs Harper, "he really took it badly last year when Janine broke up with him."

"Oh," said Mum, "I remember Janine!"

"A lovely girl. We never quite knew what went wrong: he wouldn't talk about it. But it really upset him."

"Some kind of lovers' tiff?" said Mum.

"I suppose so; these things happen. But now he's clammed right up. I'm almost sure he's seeing someone else, but I don't quite like to ask. And whoever it is he's keeping it very close to his chest. Almost as if he's…"

There was a pause. I slid a knife very carefully into the cutlery drawer.

"Not ashamed, exactly. I wouldn't go that far. But I have this strong feeling he'd rather we didn't know."

"It's probably just normal teenage secrecy," said Mum. "I can't imagine Jake doing anything foolish."

"I expect you're right. We've all kept things from our parents."

"Haven't we just!" said Mum. "I remember going out with some boy who had purple hair and tattoos all over him."

I thought, *Mum!* That was something I never knew.

"The poor boy," said Mum, "he was totally harmless! But my dad would have had an apoplexy."

"Well, this is it," said Mrs Harper. "Maybe there are some things we're better off not knowing. It is a bit worrying, though."

"Children are a worry," said Mum.

I waited to see if she was going to say anything about me, cos, I mean, if I was a worry I ought to know about it so I could do something. But Mum had obviously finished taking out rollers and brushing and spraying. The next thing I heard was her saying, "There you go! How's that?" and Mrs Harper saying, "Beautiful, as always!" I think she meant the way that Mum had done her hair rather than her herself looking beautiful, though actually she does. Her hair does, as well. It's very dark and thick like Jake's. Mum says it's a joy to work with good hair. On the other hand she says that fine hair, like Maya's, is a challenge, and she does quite like a challenge. Mine, she says, is just impossible.

"Goes its own way no matter what."

"A bit like its owner," she adds, but that is so not true! I am always going other people's way. I am very sensitive to other people and their feelings.

After we'd shut up for the night and were driving home Mum asked me if I'd heard anything about Jake having a girlfriend.

I said, "Mum! How would I know? He's a *prefect*. He's Year *Twelve*. And why, anyway?" I said.

"Mrs Harper was just a bit concerned, that's all. We'll probably be concerned about you one of these days, wondering if you're seeing anyone and if so who."

"Not me," I said. "Not for ages!"

Maya, of course, was another matter. I told her next morning, as we sat on the bus, about Mrs Harper being concerned about Jake. "She thinks he might have a girlfriend that he doesn't want her to know about... D'you think he has?" I put it as casually as I could, waiting to see what she would say.

Maya tossed her head, defiantly. "Well, if he has," she said, "it's not Hope Kennedy."

How had she discovered *that*?

"Omigod," I said, "you didn't *ask* him? You did, didn't you? You actually asked him!"

"I can ask him whatever I like," said Maya. "He doesn't mind."

I have to admit, I was curious. "So what sort of

 123 ☆

things do you talk about? When you're cadging lifts off of him."

"I don't cadge lifts off of him! Honestly," said Maya, "there are times when you can be so *horrible*. You say the meanest things just to hurt people!"

"I didn't mean to. I just wondered what you talked about."

"Anything," said Maya. "We talk about anything."

"Like whether he has a girlfriend? Maybe," I said, "I should tell his mum that *you're* his girlfriend. That would please her!"

I'd forgotten that Maya has absolutely no idea when someone is being sarcastic. Her face lit up.

"Well?" I said. "D'you think I ought?"

A little secret smile curved her lips.

"Do whatever you feel like," she said.

I looked at her through narrowed eyes. What was she hiding?

CHAPTER EIGHT

I woke up feeling quite excited on Saturday morning. For the very first time me and Maya were being trusted to go to the shopping centre on our own. Not just the little local mall off the High Street. We'd been going there for ages! It's so small that even Auntie Megs had stopped fussing that we might get lost or run into some kind of trouble. (When she said "trouble" what she actually meant was getting ourselves abducted, even though it has been drummed into us ever since I can remember that you should never, ever go anywhere with strangers.)

This Saturday I'd begged and pleaded to be allowed to go further afield.

"Can't we go to Greenfields, Mum? *Please?*"

Greenfields is out of town and so ginormous it is practically a town in itself, and Mum had been a bit hesitant at first. It was Dad that had spoken up for us.

"You can't keep them in cotton wool for ever. They've got to learn sooner or later."

Once we had Mum on our side we knew we'd won. Mum would be able to persuade Auntie Megs, no problem! Auntie Megs always follows Mum's advice. Dad said that he would drive us there and then we could get the bus back when we'd had enough.

"Unless you'd rather I came and picked you up? I can, if you like. If you don't feel confident."

I assured him that there was no need; we felt perfectly confident.

"Well, just make sure you stay together," said Mum.

"Don't worry," I said. "We'll stick like superglue!"

"And don't forget to take your phone, just in case you change your mind and want your dad to come and get you."

I said, "*Mum.* Stop behaving like Auntie Megs!"

Maya admitted to me, once we were safely in the car and on our way, that Auntie Megs had almost changed her mind at the last minute.

"She wanted to come with us! I told her, *I'm going to buy your birthday present. It's supposed to be a secret.*"

"So what are you going to buy?" I said.

"I'm going to buy a candle." Maya announced it, proudly. "A scented candle! A really *big* one, like this."

She held her hands apart, to show me. I gave a squeal.

"That's what I'm buying!" I leaned forward and tapped Dad's shoulder. "Dad, you're not to say anything."

"My lips are sealed," said Dad. "How come you've both decided on the same thing?"

"It's what we do," said Maya.

"It just happens," I said.

"It's not like we plan it."

Dad chuckled. "Great minds think alike, eh?"

It is quite strange, but it happens to be a fact that Maya and I often find we've chosen the same presents for our mums. I guess it's something to do with them being twins and me and Maya sometimes feeling like twins, even though we're so different.

"OK," said Dad, as we got out of the car. "Back home by one o'clock. You know which bus to get and where to get it?"

I said, "Yes, Dad."

"All right, all right, I'm only asking! And you've got your phone?"

I said, "Da-a-ad!"

"I've even got mine," said Maya, proudly.

"Well, that makes a change," I said as we headed

into the mall. "Let's see if there's a floor plan thingy so we can work out where to go."

I felt quite important studying the floor plan, though it didn't really help us, cos what we wanted was a candle shop and we couldn't see any.

"I s'ppose we could try in there," said Maya, jabbing a finger on the map. "Cooper's… isn't that a department store? They'd probably sell candles."

"Quick thinking!" I said.

Maya looked pleased with herself. She was even more pleased when we found the candle department, all lit up like an Aladdin's cave. We spent ages trying to decide which candles to buy. In the end Maya chose one that smelt of roses, cos of roses being Auntie Megs' favourite flower, and I chose one that smelt of violets, cos I really liked the colour. After that we had to find the card department and choose cards, and that took us for ever, as well. I was surprised, when I looked at my phone, to find that we'd been there almost an hour. Of course, we had done quite a bit of wandering about. It was a really big store and we must have been up and down the escalators at least half a dozen times.

"It's all right, we don't have to leave just yet," I said. "We can still go and have a look around outside."

We looked around so long that it was gone twelve when we finally made our way out to the bus stop – only to discover that we'd just missed a bus and the next one wasn't due for twenty minutes.

"*Bother*," I said. "I don't want to have to ring Dad!" That would be like saying we couldn't manage.

"We should have watched the time," said Maya.

Well, maybe we should have, but we hadn't.

"It's all right," I said. "We'll still be home by one o'clock. *Just*."

Maya looked doubtful. "So what shall we do while we're waiting?"

"Go and look at more shops!"

She crinkled her nose. "I'm tired of looking at shops. I don't feel like walking round any more."

Very pointedly I said, "You're not suggesting I ring Dad?"

She squirmed a bit at that, but wasn't quite brave enough to admit it was exactly what she'd been suggesting. Just as well, cos I had no intention of doing so! This was our first expedition by ourselves and we needed to prove that we could do it. Still, I didn't want to be too hard on Maya. It had shaken me a bit when she'd said about me being so horrible and saying mean things on purpose to hurt people. It had only really been this morning that we'd got back to normal – well, almost normal. I had the feeling that the least little thing and she'd accuse me of being horrible again.

"I know what we'll do," I said. "We'll go and sit down somewhere and have something to drink."

She perked up at that. "Like what?"

"I dunno! Whatever you want." I led the way back into the shopping centre. There was a coffee shop right in front of us, with a window where they sold drinks and ice creams and stuff. "Over there."

Maya rushed off, happily. "Ooh, look, they've got strawberry crush!"

I said, "Yum!" Strawberry crush, all sweet and gluggy. Enough to give our mums nightmares! "Is that what you want?"

She hesitated. "D'you think I should?"

"Why not?" I said. "Once can't hurt. And anyway it's exactly what you *ought* to have."

"Really?" She gazed at me, wide-eyed.

I said, "Strawberry *crush*?"

I waited for her to turn pink. Strawberry pink! But her gaze had suddenly flickered away. She gave a little squeal.

"Look!"

I said, "What? What?"

"Over there! It's Miss Hopwood!"

Miss Hopwood, sitting at a table just inside the cafe. Before I could stop her, Maya had gone racing over. To my way of thinking, Miss Hopwood didn't look altogether pleased to see her. *Not* very surprising. I'm sure teachers have enough of us at school without being made to put up with us in their free time.

By the time I reluctantly caught up with her, Maya was actually sitting down at Miss Hopwood's table. I would never have had the nerve! Of course I'd forgotten, though, about her running the Music Club. I heard Miss Hopwood say, "Oh, Maya, of course you can try out for the choir! An excellent idea. Hallo, Mattie! Are you here on a shopping trip?"

"We've been buying presents for our mums' birthday," said Maya. "We've got scented candles!"

"Lovely," said Miss Hopwood. "I'm afraid I've gone and overdone it... I've been shopping till I'm dropping!" She waved a hand at some bags on the seat next to her. "Not very sensible when you have to struggle home on the bus."

"We're going home on the bus," said Maya.

"Yes, but you haven't stupidly burdened yourself with all these bags! I should have exercised a bit of restraint, not having my car with me." She pulled a face. "Wouldn't start, would it? Heaven knows what's wrong with it; I'm not very good with cars."

I smiled, politely. It's always weird seeing a teacher out of school, especially when they're young and trendy like Miss Hopwood. I mean, she didn't *look* like a teacher. She probably felt it was a bit weird seeing me and Maya out of school. I felt pretty sure she'd rather not.

"I was thinking," she confessed, "that I might have to grit my teeth and take a cab back. Fortunately I bumped into a very kind young gentleman who's offered me a lift."

Miss Hopwood looked up, and smiled. Me and Maya also looked up.

"Hallo, you two," said Jake. He seemed a bit… well! Taken aback. I did *so* hope he didn't think we'd come here on purpose to stalk him. "What brings you to this neck of the woods?"

"They've been buying scented candles for their mums," said Miss Hopwood. "I was just telling them how I was going to have to fight my way back on the bus and how you'd come to my rescue!"

"Ooh!" Maya sprang up and clasped her hands together like she was praying. "D'you think you could come to our rescue, as well?"

Jake shook his head. "Sorry, kiddo! No can do. I've already promised Miss Hopwood I'll give her a lift home."

"That's all right," twinkled Maya. "We don't mind if you drop her off first."

Omigod, I nearly died. I don't think I have ever been more ashamed in my life. I felt like crawling under the table and curling into a ball.

"It's OK," I said. "We're getting the bus!"

"But we'll be late," wailed Maya. "We should have left ages go! We'll never get back by one o'clock. My mum's going to go crazy!"

"No, she won't, we can—" I was about to say we could just ring her and explain, no problem, but I didn't get it out fast enough.

"Maya's mum is a bit of a worrier," agreed Jake.

"In that case —" Miss Hopwood pushed her chair back — "we must certainly give you a lift! We can drop the girls off first," she said. "Make sure they're back in good time."

"We *will* be," I said. "There's a bus in just a few minutes."

"You mean, like, a quarter of an hour," said Maya.

"No, no, no, we can't have that," said Miss Hopwood. "That would certainly be cutting it a bit fine. Come on! Let's get you home."

Miss Hopwood reached out for her bags, but Jake got there before her.

"Here," he said. "Let me."

They really didn't look that heavy. Clothes, I thought they probably were. But Jake was always very polite. Unlike Maya. I thought it was really rude of her to say we wouldn't mind if Jake dropped Miss Hopwood off first. I mean, Miss Hopwood was a *teacher*. Of course she had to be dropped off first! It wasn't up to Maya to tell Jake what he could and couldn't do.

She bounced along beside him as we made our way to the car park. I was left to follow with Miss Hopwood, but I could hear Maya prattling on, telling him how we'd both bought scented candles for our mums and how Miss Hopwood had said she could try out for the choir. Miss Hopwood obviously heard as well.

"Maya's really come on this term, hasn't she?" she said. "She used to be such a quiet little thing! I was so pleased when she joined the Music Club. She's definitely starting to blossom. Don't you think?"

I said yes, cos what else could I say? I couldn't very well tell Miss Hopwood that Maya had this huge enormous crush and the only reason she'd joined the Music Club was cos Jake was a member. I did add, though, that I didn't really think she could sing.

"None of us can, in our family."

"Well, that's all right," said Miss Hopwood. "I'm just pleased she feels confident enough to give it a go."

"It was Jake's idea," I said.

We both directed our gaze for a moment at the two of them, Jake striding ahead with Maya trit-trotting to keep up with him.

"He's known Maya since she was little," I said. "He's known both of us, actually." And then, feeling some sort of apology was called for, I added, "Sometimes it makes her take advantage of him."

Miss Hopwood smiled, tolerantly. "Well, I'm sure he's very easy to take advantage of."

"But she shouldn't have asked for a lift," I said. "Not when he'd already offered to give you one."

"Oh, Mattie, don't worry about it," said Miss Hopwood. "Anything to stop her mum worrying. I'm in no particular rush."

I was appalled, when we got to the car park, to find that Maya had already installed herself in the front seat. It was so *rude*. Miss Hopwood was a teacher; she should have had the front seat!

Maya sat there, clutching her scented candle and beaming angelically.

"Don't you think you ought to come in the back?" I said.

"I can't," said Maya. "I'll get sick."

"You didn't get sick this morning," I said. She'd sat quite happily in the back of Dad's car.

"That was different," said Maya. "I'd just had breakfast. Now I'm *empty*."

"Another reason to get you back home," said Jake. "Hop in, Mattie!"

"So are we going to drop Miss Hopwood off first?" said Maya as we moved off down the ramp.

What did she mean, *we*? Like she had any say in the matter!

"No, I'm going to drop you two girls off first," said Jake, "and then I'll take Miss Hopwood home."

"It wouldn't bother us –" Maya assured him of it, earnestly – "if you wanted to do it the other way round."

I felt myself cringing. What did it take to stop her? Miss Hopwood did her best.

"Maya, it's all right," she said. "I live way out in Forestdale, right over the other side of town. I'm really putting poor Jake to a lot of inconvenience."

"So if he took you first," argued Maya, "he wouldn't have to drive all the way out to Forestdale and then all the way back again. It'd make far more sense!"

"Yes, and it would make you late for your deadline," said Jake. "And then your mum would start to panic."

"Oh, that doesn't matter." Maya dismissed her mum, airily. "I've got my phone. I could ring her! Shall I ring her?"

Oh, yes, she could ring her all right *now*. Now that she'd got her way and was sitting in the car next to Jake.

"Shall I?" said Maya.

"*No.*" I leaned forward, threateningly. "I told Dad we'd be home by one o'clock and we're going to be home by one o'clock!"

But honestly," said Maya, "w—"

"Maya, please," begged Miss Hopwood. "You're

beginning to make me feel really guilty. Maybe Jake should just drop me off at the nearest bus stop?"

"No way," said Jake. "Maya's going to behave herself. *Isn't* she?"

I thought for a moment that what she was going to do was sulk, but instead she gave him this impish smile and said, "If you say so."

"I do say so. That's better! OK, let's get going. We'll have you home in no time."

CHAPTER NINE

"Honestly," I said, "it was just *so* embarrassing. She actually told Jake that we wouldn't mind if he dropped Miss Hopwood off first!"

Cate pulled a face. "That is some cheek."

"I didn't know where to look! I felt like digging a hole and burying myself."

"Poor you," said Cate.

We were doing our usual wander round the field after lunch. Lucy and Nasreen weren't there, and I was glad about that. Although we are all good friends, Cate is the one I am closest to. She is the one I confide in. She is always so calm and full of good advice.

"It made me feel really ashamed," I said.

Cate nodded. "Cos of being her cousin and feeling responsible."

"Exactly!" Cate understood. It is why she is my best friend: you don't have to spell things out. "It was like –" I waved a hand – "like *I* was saying we wouldn't mind. Like I was agreeing with her!"

"Hm." Cate regarded me, thoughtfully. "You do know," she said, "that you're not *actually* responsible? You can't stop her saying things! Any more than you can stop her behaving the way she does. It's not your fault."

I said, "I know it's not my *fault*, but it still makes us both look ridiculous."

I didn't want to look ridiculous in front of Jake. *Or* Miss Hopwood. But mostly Jake.

"You should have seen her in the car! Like a spoilt brat. Almost, like, *flirting* with him."

I was thinking of that little smile she'd given him. He should have squashed her. Right there and then. *And* he should have made her get out of the car and come and sit in the back. That was where she belonged; not up front with him. It was just encouraging her.

"I do get that it's annoying," said Cate.

I said, "It's not just annoying; it makes me cringe! And he never does *anything* to stop her."

"Is that why it upsets you so much? Cos he lets her get away with it?"

"I just don't think he should encourage her," I said.

"No." Cate thought about it for a moment. "Would it still bother you, d'you think, if it was someone else?"

I frowned. What did she mean by that?

"Like if it was anybody except Jake? Would it still bother you? Or is it just cos it's him?"

I felt my cheeks grow hot and pink. What was she saying? It was bad enough Maya accusing me of feeling jealous. But *Cate*? I could forgive Maya cos of her being in the "throes", as Mum called it. All eaten up with her mad passion. But Cate was my best friend! She ought to know better.

"It's perfectly understandable," said Cate. "I'm not blaming you! Nobody likes to look ridiculous, especially in front of someone like – well, I mean, Jake Harper! Let's face it… half the girls in school have probably got a crush on him."

"That's got nothing to do with it," I said, crossly. "I'm just worried for Maya! In case she goes and does something *really* stupid, like…"

"Like what?"

"I don't know! But he's *eighteen*. What if he…"

"What?"

"If he…"

"Takes advantage? I'm sure he wouldn't," said Cate. "Not Jake!"

"But you were the one that said he might fancy her, cos of her being so pretty!"

"I didn't say he'd actually *do* anything."

"Then why does he keep encouraging her?"

"Boys can't help it," said Cate. "They like being flirted with. So do girls," she added. "There isn't any harm in just flirting."

"I bet you wouldn't say that if it was Immy!" Immy is her little sister. "I bet you wouldn't be so happy if she was flirting with him! Cramming into the front seat and simpering at him and making eyes and—"

"OK!" She flung up a hand, like, *enough.* "Maybe I would be just a *tiny* bit bothered."

I said, "Right! So what would you do about it?"

"I'd… talk to her," said Cate.

"Talk to her!" I made a scoffing sound. "You really think you can talk to someone when they're in her state?"

"You could try."

"I have tried! She won't listen. She just gets cross and accuses me of saying mean things."

And of being jealous. Which I so was *not.*

Cate said, "Well… OK! In that case…"

I waited, expectantly, for words of wisdom.

"What I would do," said Cate, "I'd talk to my mum. After all, it's what mums are for. And yours is really nice!"

I said, "I know, but…"

"What's the problem? Tell your mum! Let her deal with it. Simple!"

It may have seemed simple to Cate, but to me it seemed like a sort of betrayal. How could I go to Mum behind Maya's back? Telling her that Maya had a crush was one thing. Telling her I was worried something might actually happen was quite another. Mum would feel bound to tell Auntie Megs and that would make Auntie Megs fly into one of her panics and then what would happen? Maya would accuse me of betraying her. She would hate me for ever more! I tried explaining this to Cate. She listened sympathetically. She knew all about Auntie Megs and her panic attacks and Uncle Kev and his weird ideas.

"Still, I really think you ought to do something," she urged. "I mean, if you're that worried. Maybe you should go to *Jake's* mum?"

I recoiled, in horror. I couldn't go running to Jake's mum! "She already knows," I said. "My mum's already told her Maya's got this massive crush."

"But does she know how far it's gone? Does she know he's letting her flirt with him?"

"N-no, but..." He might not even realise that she was flirting with him! He might just feel sorry for her. I wouldn't want to get him into any sort of trouble.

Cate could obviously see that I was reluctant.

"P'raps what you ought to do," she said, "is try talking to Maya again. Tell her that she's making herself look ridiculous and if it doesn't stop you'll have to tell someone. Not cos you're being horrible, but because you're worried. That's what I think you ought to do."

I heaved a sigh. "I suppose."

"Well, you've got to do something," said Cate.

I knew that I had. I wasn't very happy at the thought of talking to Maya, but anything was better than talking to Jake's mum.

"This evening," urged Cate. "Get it over with!"

I so didn't want to. I knew what would happen. Maya would get all sulky and defiant. She might even accuse me again of being jealous. Maybe, I thought, I could leave it till the weekend? Not that it would be any *better* at the weekend, but – well! Anything could happen between then and now. Uncle Kev might suddenly reappear, or at least do something to get in touch. That would cheer her up! It might even take her mind off Jake – who probably *wasn't* actually encouraging her. It was probably just my imagination. I do have a very active imagination. Really, the more I came to think about it the more I thought it would probably be better if I *didn't* talk to Maya. The last thing I wanted to do was put ideas into her head. Not if it was all totally innocent.

Relief flooded over me. Cate had it wrong! Talking to Maya was not only unnecessary, but would in fact be a big mistake. Well, that is what I told myself, until that stupid, idiotic, *irritating* Linzi had to go and put her clumping great foot in it. We were waiting at the bus stop at the end of school, me and Maya and a few others, when the creature suddenly arrived and plonked itself down next to us.

"Excuse me," I said. "Did you know there was a queue?"

"Oh!" She dismissed it, airily. "There'll be room for everyone."

Serve her right if there was a riot. You can't just push in front of people like that! Except if you're Linzi Baxter you obviously can.

"So." She gave Maya this searching look. "Not getting a lift from your boyfriend?"

Maya's face grew instantly pink with pleasure. *Boyfriend*. It was just playing right into her fantasies.

"He couldn't today. He has things to do."

"You actually asked him?" I said.

She tossed her head. "I didn't have to!"

What did *that* mean? It niggled at me all the way home.

I couldn't find out, because of Linzi being there, but it niggled and niggled and kept on niggling even when I got in. Maya would never have had the nerve to speak to Anil the way she spoke to Jake! She would never have dared ask *him* why he hadn't been there last time she'd gone into the store, or what he was doing at the weekend, or whether he was going to be there tomorrow. With Anil she had been all shy and giggly and bashful. With Jake she was positively bold.

On the other hand, suppose she hadn't asked him? Suppose he'd told her without being asked? Like, *Hi, kiddo! Sorry I can't give you a lift this afternoon, I've got something to do.*

In some ways that would be even worse, cos that would mean it wasn't just Maya being bold, but Jake actually taking the trouble to go and talk to her.

Actually seeking her out. Explaining why he couldn't give her a lift. Why would he do that? It wasn't like she needed a lift; he knew that she always came home with me, on the bus. It was all starting to get a little bit worrying.

If Mum had been there when I got back I might almost have done what Cate had urged me to do. I might have confided in her and then at least it would have been a weight off my shoulders. If Mum decided to go rushing off to alert Auntie Megs – well! Too bad. It would serve Maya right for getting all angry and accusing me of things.

But Mum was still at work and only Dad was there, and I never feel I can confide in Dad the way I can with Mum. Dad really does tend to get a bit impatient with poor Auntie Megs and he isn't always very sympathetic towards Maya. So I couldn't talk to Dad.

But I was beginning to have this very intense feeling that Cate was right: I had to do *something*.

In the end I snatched up my phone and called Maya.

I did it quite suddenly, without any warning, taking myself by surprise so I wouldn't have time to think myself out of it. Maya picked up immediately, which was just as well since otherwise I most probably would have got cold feet and switched off.

Maya shrieked, "Mattie! I'm so glad it's you! Do you understand this maths homework Miss Cowell gave us? Cos I don't! What is three minus two and five over nine? What's it supposed to mean?"

For a moment I couldn't imagine what on earth she was talking about. And then it came to me: "You mean three minus two-and-five-ninths?"

"I don't know!" She sounded aggrieved. "I can't make any sense of it!"

"It's what we were doing just the other day."

"I didn't understand it *then*," said Maya.

"So why didn't you say?"

She ignored that. "There's loads of it! What am I going to do?"

I sighed. "D'you want me to come over?"

"Oh, Mattie, would you? *Please?*"

I told Dad that I was going round to Maya's to help her with her homework and went rushing off before he could start grumbling about it being "high time she learnt to do it for herself". Like I said, Dad is not always sympathetic. Auntie Megs, on the other hand, when I explained why I had come, was ever so grateful. She said, "Oh, Mattie, that is so kind of you! Poor Maya does struggle! I just don't know what she'd do without you."

Rather gruffly, cos it was a bit embarrassing, I said, "That's OK. I don't mind. I quite like maths."

"I'm afraid Maya takes after me," said Auntie Megs. "She just doesn't have a mathematical turn of mind."

According to Dad, she didn't make any effort. But that is just Dad.

I found Maya in her bedroom, sitting cross-legged on the bed with Poppy sprawled across her lap.

"So where's your homework?" I said.

She pulled a face. "Under the bed. It fell down there

and I couldn't disturb Poppy, and anyway you said you were going to come round, so…"

"I'm not going to *do* it for you," I said. "I'm going to explain it to you and then you can get on and do it yourself."

"Yes." She sat upright, trying her best to look studious. Not easy when you have a dog lying all over you, waving its paws in the air.

Sternly I said, "You can't work with Poppy on top of you. *I'll* have Poppy; you pick up your maths book."

By the time we'd been through all the questions I was feeling quite worn out. It is an uphill struggle, trying to get Maya to grasp any sort of mathematical concept.

"I hope you understand a bit better now," I said.

She assured me that she did. "You make it all so clear. You're ever so much better than Miss Cowell."

I said, "Huh!"

"So, anyway," said Maya, "what was it you were ringing about?"

"Oh! Yes. Well." I pulled at Poppy's ears. "I just – well! I just wanted…"

"What, what?"

But it was too late; the moment had gone. I'd had too much time to think about it.

Brightly I said, "You know next week? It's half term? Did I tell you, we're going up to Sheffield to see my cousins?"

"Yes, you said," said Maya.

"Did I? Oh! I wasn't sure."

"You said it made you feel guilty cos of me not having any."

"You've got me!"

"Apart from you. You said it made you feel bad." She was right: I did sometimes feel bad about it. It seemed hard on Maya, my dad coming from a large family and me having not only a gran and grandad but lots of aunts and uncles and cousins. Maya didn't have anyone, other than me and Mum. Uncle Kev had been brought up in foster homes and had never even known his mum and dad.

"It's a pity you can't come with us," I said.

"That would mean leaving Mum," said Maya.

"So maybe you could both come!"

She shook her head. "Your dad wouldn't like that."

Unfortunately it was true: he wouldn't. It made me feel even more guilty. Maya isn't stupid; she knows that Dad gets impatient with Auntie Megs.

"It's all right," she said, "I couldn't come anyway. I've arranged to see Tansy and Bella. We're all stuck here so I expect we'll maybe have a sleepover."

"Oh, well, good," I said. "That's good!"

There was a bit of a pause. Maya pulled Poppy back on to her lap.

"So is that all you were ringing for?"

"Yes! Well – n-no. Not exactly." Idly, trying to distract myself, I picked up Maya's phone, which was lying on the bed, and started flicking through the photos she had on it. Auntie Megs, Uncle Kev; Poppy, me; Tansy, Bella and, omigod! She had a photo of Jake. She had *two* photos of Jake.

"Where did you get these?" I said.

She leaned across to peer at the phone. "It's Jake."

"I can see it's Jake! When did you take them?"

"I dunno. Can't remember."

"*Honestly*," I said.

She looked at me, innocently. "Honestly what?"

"Honestly, how could you?"

"There's no law against taking photos!"

"Did he know you were taking them?"

"Yes – no! Maybe. I don't know. *What's your problem?*"

I took a deep breath. "You know what my problem is."

"Oh!" cried Maya. "Not that again!"

I said, "Yes. *That* again. You can't carry on like this! You're making yourself look ridiculous; it's just not right! He can't ever be your boyfriend. You know that, don't you? Really and truly, deep down… you know it's not possible!"

Her eyes slid away from me.

"Maya," I said, "he's *eighteen*."

I braced myself for the outburst – *you're so mean,*

you're so horrible, you're just jealous! – but it never came. She stared across at me, her eyes very big and blue and filled with tragic tears. I found myself thinking how pretty she was, and wishing, just for a moment, that I could be pretty, too. It doesn't usually bother me, or at any rate I refuse to let it; but suddenly I saw all too clearly why Jake was so tolerant and how it was she got away with things.

"Maya," I said, "I'm not having a go at you! Really I'm not. It's just…"

"I can't help it!" Her voice rose in a despairing wail. "I love him! And he loves me!"

CHAPTER TEN

I stared at her, helplessly. Did she really believe that? I didn't know what to say. I was a bit shaken, to tell the truth. I'd expected her to be defiant; I hadn't expected her to go all tragic on me.

She tightened her arms around Poppy. "You don't know what it's like! You've never been in love. It hurts! It hurts so much! It's no good looking at me like that, cos there's nothing I can do about it. You don't get to choose who you fall in love with; it's something that just happens. You wouldn't know," she said. She choked as a fresh spurt of tears went streaming down her cheeks. "You're always so *sensible!*" She made it sound like it was some kind of character flaw.

I said, "Well, if I am it's just the way I'm made."

Very fiercely Maya said, "Yes, and this is the way I'm made! I have *feelings.*"

"I have feelings," I said. "I have feelings for you! I don't want anything bad to happen."

"Like what?"

"Well… like you getting hurt. I'm not being mean," I said, "honestly! I'm just telling it like it is."

"You don't know how it is." She buried her face in Poppy's fur. "You don't understand!"

"I'm trying to," I said.

I could tell she didn't think I was trying hard enough.

"Anyway." I slid off the bed. "That's what I came to say. I'm going to go, now."

She didn't make any attempt to stop me. She didn't even come downstairs to see me off. It was Auntie Megs who thanked me for coming.

"All done?" she said. "Did you manage to get through to her?"

"I hope so," I said.

"Well, I'm sure you did your best! Your poor mum used to spend hours with me, trying to explain things. Not a bit of use!" Auntie Megs laughed, happily. "I'm a complete moron when it comes to figures. But honestly, Mattie, it was so good of you to drop by."

"That's all right," I said.

I just wished I could feel more confident – even just a *little* bit confident – that Maya would take some notice of what I'd said, but it seems when people are in love they simply lose all the common sense they ever had. Not that Maya had ever had that much in the first place. Unlike me, who obviously had far too much and probably wouldn't ever manage to fall in love. A bleak prospect!

Next day at school Cate was eager to know what had happened.

"Did you do anything?"

I told her that I had talked to Maya again.

"Did she get mad at you?"

I said, "No, she started crying and said they were in love and it hurt and she couldn't do anything about it."

Cate looked alarmed. "She really thinks he's in love with her?"

"That's what she said."

"Do *you* think he is?"

I hesitated. Surely he couldn't be? But what did I know? I wasn't an expert on the way boys' minds work.

Cate's brow wrinkled. "So what happens now? Are you going to talk to your mum?"

I said, "No, cos it's half term next week. They won't be seeing each other." Not in school, at any rate.

Surely not even Maya would be bold enough to call round?

"I'll wait till we come back," I said. "If she's still in a state I'll… I'll do something then!" Have a word with Mum. That's what I would do. But not before half term, cos I didn't want to spoil our trip to Sheffield. "Truly," I promised, "I will!"

I still thought it was sad that Maya couldn't come with us. If it hadn't been for Uncle Kev she could have done, cos if he'd been home she wouldn't have minded leaving her mum. And Dad surely couldn't object to just Maya?

But it wasn't to be, and by the time we arrived in Sheffield, with Auntie Suzie throwing open the door to welcome us, I'd almost forgotten about her. I might as well admit it, I hardly thought of her at all the whole time we were there. It's always such fun at Auntie Suzie's! There is Uncle Ted, who is very big and jolly, and Shona, who is the same age as me, and Rob, who is two years older. There was also Owen, who is Rob's best friend. A whole bunch of us! We spent almost the whole time going on day trips to places like the Wildlife Park and the Butterfly House and Alton Towers. It was probably a bit selfish of me, but nothing could have been further from my mind than what Maya might be up to.

There was only one occasion when I really stopped and thought about her. That was when we were riding one of the roller coasters at Alton Towers and Owen reached out and gripped my hand, really hard. I said, "I'm not frightened!" and he grinned and said, "No, but I am." Of course I didn't believe him, especially when we got off and he still stayed by my side, paying special attention to me, all the time we were there – and then got into Dad's car on the way home so he could sit next to me. I noticed Mum and Auntie Suzie exchanging these glances and giving these little amused smiles. It was a bit embarrassing, but I didn't mind. It was the very first time I had ever felt that a boy... well... fancied me! I couldn't help being relieved that Maya *hadn't* been able to come with us, cos who would ever fancy someone like me, with my bristle brush hair and face like a doughnut (in other words, *round*), when they could have Maya, who is so tiny and fragile and pretty?

We didn't get back home till really late on Sunday night. Mum was fussing cos of me having school next day, but Dad said, for goodness' sake, what did it matter, just for once? I certainly wasn't bothered! My brain was still all fizzing and buzzing, so that I began to wonder if I might have been a bit hard on Maya. Maybe this was what it was like, falling in love? Though of course, as I reminded myself, there was absolutely nothing wrong falling in love with a boy of fourteen. There was *everything* wrong falling in love with a boy of Jake's age! But I really couldn't think about that now. It was gone midnight when we arrived home and I was quite happy for Mum to hustle me straight upstairs. I would check with Maya in the morning. See how she was getting on.

Next morning, not surprisingly, Mum had to call me

three times before I finally managed to unglue my eyes and fall out of bed. I ended up in a mad rush, tearing off to the bus stop, still trying to cram my last piece of toast into my mouth. I arrived, panting, at exactly the same moment as the bus. And there was no one there! That is, Linzi was there, but no Maya.

"Where's she got to?" said Linzi.

"I don't know." I stared round, helplessly. Not a sign of her!

"So you getting on, or what?"

I didn't really have much choice. The next bus wasn't due for another twenty minutes. It would make me late and that would ruin my record, cos so far that term I'd been one hundred per cent punctual. Mrs Croft, our year group tutor, had even congratulated me.

Linzi said, "*Well?*"

I said, "Yes, OK."

I sprang on to the bus and the doors clamped shut. There was still no sign of Maya. It wasn't like her to be late! I had threatened her too often with dire consequences. What could be keeping her?

I peered out of the window, hoping to see her racing towards the bus stop, but still nothing.

"She's going to be really late," said Linzi, in tones of satisfaction. "She'll cop it!"

"I'll give her a ring," I said.

I tried, but she didn't answer. Probably left her phone somewhere. *Again*. I sent her a text, which she almost certainly wouldn't pick up, but there wasn't much more I could do.

"Maybe she's run off with her boyfriend," said Linzi. She gave a little titter. "Then she'll really be for it!"

Or more likely Jake would be.

Linzi looked at me hopefully.

"You think she has?"

"Of course not!" I snapped. "That's a ludicrous idea."

Auntie Megs would have been on the phone to Mum in an instant.

"She's probably just overslept," I said.

"You reckon?"

"Well, I did," I said. "I thought I wasn't going to make it."

Linzi said, "Hm." She didn't sound convinced. It was like she actually *wanted* Maya to have run off. I suppose in a way I couldn't blame her. School life can sometimes be so dreary, what with the same old lessons and the same old teachers, day in, day out, that you just long for something exciting to happen. Not that it would be exciting for poor Auntie Megs, and it wouldn't be very exciting for Jake, either. He would be in serious trouble.

As we reached the school gates I saw Maya's friend Tansy walking ahead of us and ran to catch up with her.

"Did you see Maya over half term?"

"No." Tansy pulled a face. "She was supposed to be coming on Saturday for a sleepover with me and Bella, but she sent a text saying she couldn't make it."

"Oh." My heart almost stopped. "Did she say why?"

Tansy shook her head. "Bella says we're lucky she even thought to text. You know how scatty she is."

Irresponsible, Dad would have said. Like Uncle Kev.

Cate was waiting for me in the classroom, eager to tell me about the camping trip she'd been on and to politely inquire if I'd had a good time up in Sheffield. I said, "Yes, it was amazing." Cate said, "So was camping. You'll never believe what happened!"

She proceeded to tell me in minute detail, but even though I did my best to show a proper interest Cate wasn't fooled. She knows me too well.

"What's wrong?" she said. "You've gone all vacant!"

I just had time to hiss, "Maya's not here," when the bell rang for Monday morning assembly and we all had to go stomping off, single file in deathly silence, to the hall. If we didn't go in single file there would be pile-ups and traffic chaos, and if we didn't maintain deathly silence the noise would be intolerable. That, at any rate, is what Mrs Croft says as she watches over us with her beady eyes, ears alert for the faintest rustle.

"Maya's not here?" whispered Cate.

"She wasn't at the bus stop. I don't know where she is! She's not answering her phone."

"So what...?"

"I don't know!" I swivelled round in search of Tansy or Bella. Bella caught me looking at her and raised her eyebrows. "Have you heard anything from Maya?" I mouthed at her. She frowned and mouthed back at me: *What?*

"Bella! Mattie!" Mrs Croft put a bony finger to her lips. "Stop talking!"

We subsided, instantly. Mrs Croft is not someone you argue with. She is horribly strict.

The hall had started to fill up, Years Seven and Eight down at the front. The prefects were already there, sitting on chairs along one side. I craned my head, checking that Jake was where he should be. Cate craned with me. We turned, to look at each other. Jake wasn't there! Cate slowly shook her head. Not exactly accusing; more like reproachful. *You really should have done something!* But what? I'd talked to Maya! If she didn't listen, it was hardly my fault.

Desperately, I swivelled round so that I could see to the end of the hall, where people were still filing in. Jake was not amongst them.

That was the moment when my heart went cold. No Jake. No Maya. *Where were they both?*

The hall door opened again and I shot back round, but it was only a teacher coming in late.

"Hey!" Further down the line, Linzi was leaning forward, flapping a hand to gain my attention.

"What?" I mouthed it at her, irritably. She jerked her head towards Jake's empty chair.

"Where is he?"

How was I supposed to know? I wasn't his keeper! Any more than I was Maya's. Oh, but Auntie Megs would be devastated if she'd gone and done something stupid! And even if it wasn't my fault I'd still feel terrible.

I swivelled again, but the hall doors had been closed. Mrs Croft, at the end of the row, hissed angrily at me.

"Mattie! Just keep still and stop fidgeting."

Assembly only lasts for about ten minutes, but that day it seemed to go on for ever. I sat there, rigid, not daring to do any more swivelling. Cate squeezed my hand.

"It mightn't be what you think."

But if that was the case, where were they? Maya's despairing cry still rang in my ears: "I love him! I love him so much! And he loves me!"

I hadn't believed her. I'd thought she was fooling herself, and that Jake was just being kind.

By the time assembly was over I had already lived out in my mind the terrible scene where I had to break the news to Auntie Megs, when I would have to admit that Maya was so head over heels in love she would have done anything, gone anywhere, just to be with Jake – and that I had done nothing to stop her. I had simply sat back and let it happen.

I think, honestly, that I have never been so worried in my life. I had already made up my mind that I would have to go to the office and ask permission to ring Mum. Not Auntie Megs; I couldn't face that. But Mum. Mum would know what to do! Even if it meant going to the police. *Me* going to the police. Answering questions. Telling them about Jake. Omigod, Jake! What would they do to him? If he and Maya had run off, what would they do? They might arrest him! They might call it abduction. It could ruin his entire life! All for one moment of madness. Unless he really did love her? But she was only twelve years old. It was a crime to run away with someone who was only twelve years old! Why, oh why, hadn't I said something sooner? All these thoughts were racing helter-skelter round my head as we filed back to our classrooms. Jake – Maya – ring Mum – the police…

And then, suddenly, Cate was gripping my arm.

"What?" I said. "What?"

Silently, she pointed. *Oh!* I plunged forward.

"Maya!"

* * *

She was there, sitting at her desk, looking like a cat that has been at the cream. Not a hint of concern that she'd missed assembly and was going to be in big trouble. I rushed up to her.

"Where have you been? Why are you so late?"

She gave me this radiant smile. "We only just got back. We nearly didn't come at all!"

I could feel myself gaping, my mouth hanging open. What was she saying?

"We went to Brighton! We spent the whole week there. We stayed in this hotel sort of place. It was so fun! I didn't ever want to come back."

I stared at her, appalled. Cate flashed me this quick glance. Linzi, brash as ever, said, "Brighton! Well, that's original."

Maya looked at her, earnestly. "It's lovely! I've never been there before."

"Oh, it's the place to go," said Linzi.

She had this silly know-it-all grin on her face. Maya, on the other hand, was beaming. What did she have to beam about? Didn't she realise the trouble Jake could be in?

"Brighton," Linzi solemnly assured us, "is where it's all at."

"Yes!" Maya stared round, obviously very pleased with herself. "That's exactly what Dad said!"

Dad? Relief came flooding over me in a great wave. "You went with Uncle Kev? When did he…? I mean, why did you…? I mean…"

Maya laughed, happily. "He came back! Sunday morning. He just turned up, with this friend he'd met, and the friend has a car and Dad said, let's all go down to Brighton to celebrate, and—"

"Celebrate what?" I was totally bewildered. I could see that Cate was, too.

"Dad's new plan!" Maya brought it out triumphantly. "He and his friend Ken? The one he just met? They're going to start a doggy hotel and they're going to call it Pampered Pooches. People will be able to leave their dogs there when they go on holiday and Dad said I can help look after them. We could take them for walks," said Maya. "You and me! Dad would pay us for it. He wouldn't expect us to do it for nothing."

I listened, bemused, as Maya prattled on. She was so joyous I didn't want to burst her bubble by pointing out that not a single one of Uncle Kev's ideas had ever come to anything. In any case I was feeling too joyous myself. All that worry, all for nothing!

Even better she seemed to have forgotten about Jake; at any rate she showed no inclination to go and hang around the car park when we left school at the end of the day, waiting to cadge a lift. If she had I might have told her that he wasn't in school, unless he'd arrived mid-morning, but she didn't even bother to look in the direction of the car park. Instead, she burbled non-stop all the way up the road, telling me about Brighton and about the hotel they'd stayed in and how they'd gone on the pier and Uncle Kev had taken her on the bumper cars and they'd walked along the front at night and had fish and chips and then gone back on the pier again, and Uncle Kev's friend Ken had won a stuffed toy and had given it to her, and they'd even managed to persuade Auntie Megs to go on the ghost train, and honestly it had been so fun!

I could see that it must have been. Linzi would no doubt have sneered, being the sort of person that went off to places like Marbella for *her* holidays, but Maya hardly ever went away anywhere with her mum and dad and she was absolutely bubbling over with excitement.

Next day was when she'd normally have gone to the Music Club. I asked her if she was still going to go and she said, "Oh! Yes. I'd forgotten. I'm not really sure classical's my sort of music."

"It's been cancelled, anyway," said Emily, happening to overhear. "Miss Hopwood's off sick."

"Oh, dear," said Maya. "She was going to audition me for the choir."

"Honestly," I said, "I don't know why you're bothering. You know we're both practically tone deaf!"

"Yes." Maya sighed. "I suppose you're right. I probably wouldn't have got in."

In spite of the sigh, she didn't sound too regretful.

A couple of days later Jake was back in school, but Maya plainly wasn't obsessed any more. I couldn't help feeling it was a bit odd that one minute she could be so deep in love it hurt and the next minute all she could talk about was Brighton and Uncle Kev's new project. But maybe, I thought, that was what happened when you fell in love. You could fall out of it just as quickly as you'd fallen in. How would I know? It had never happened to me.

CHAPTER ELEVEN

It was a week later when Linzi self-importantly came up to us (us being me and Maya) to ask if we'd heard the rumour.

I said, "What rumour?" I tried not to show too much interest as it doesn't do to encourage her. She is always hearing rumours. Most of them turn out to be totally unfounded, but she still can't resist telling people. Any more, I suppose, than people can resist listening. It is only human nature.

"Are you sure you really want to know?" she said, darting a sideways glance at Maya.

Why wouldn't we? Why ask?

"It's just…" She put a hand up to the side of her face and swivelled her eyes fiercely in Maya's direction, at the same time contorting her features as if in some kind of agony. What *was* she playing at? "It's about Miss Hopwood," she said.

"What about her?"

"You probably think she's off sick."

"That's what Emily said." And Emily, unlike Linzi, didn't deal in rumours.

Linzi smiled, pityingly. "Emily just believes what she's told."

"You mean you've been told something different?"

"I know the truth," said Linzi. "Some people –" the eyes swivelled again – "might already have guessed."

"Guessed what?" said Maya, suddenly waking up.

"The truth!"

"About what?"

"Your boyfriend."

"I thought it was about Miss Hopwood," said Maya, looking puzzled.

"It's about both of them."

I said, "What d'you mean, both of them?"

"Only ran off together, didn't they?"

There was a startled silence.

"Ran off where?" said Maya.

"Well, it wasn't Brighton."

You really cannot help wanting to strangle that girl. She is just so *utterly* annoying.

"So where was it?" I said.

"France." She brought it out with an air of triumph.

Maya said, "*France?*"

"Spent the week there."

"Jake and Miss Hopwood?"

"Yup." Linzi nodded. Obviously very satisfied with herself.

I glanced anxiously at Maya. "It's only a stupid rumour," I said.

"I'm just telling you what I heard," said Linzi.

"From who?"

Linzi shrugged. "It's what people are saying. It's why Miss Hopwood hasn't come back."

"So where is she?"

"Been suspended."

"Oh, and she was going to audition me for the choir!" wailed Maya.

"No, she wasn't," I snapped. "You'd already decided not to bother."

"Well, but I don't understand... why have they suspended her?"

"Cos she broke the rules," said Linzi. "Teachers aren't allowed to do that sort of thing."

"What about Jake?"

"He's all right. He's not a teacher."

Maya fell silent, biting her lip. A week ago, if anyone had told her that Jake had run off with somebody she would have been plunged into the depths of abject misery. Now she just seemed concerned that he wasn't in trouble.

"It's still only a rumour," I said.

"It's true," insisted Linzi. She nodded at Maya. "*She* knows."

"She doesn't know any more than you do! It's just gossip." I grabbed Maya by the arm. "Let's go!" We didn't have to stand there and listen to Linzi spreading malicious rumours. "I don't believe a word of it," I said as I hustled us off. "Jake and Miss Hopwood? It's ridiculous!"

I expected Maya to agree with me. *Of course* it was ridiculous. Miss Hopwood was a teacher! Instead, to my surprise she said, "D'you remember that day we saw him in his car with someone and you thought it was Hope?"

"Not really," I said.

"Well, you did," said Maya. "She had blonde hair and you said it looked like Hope, and I was so-o-o jealous. I'm surprised you don't remember."

Taking a chance, I said, "Have you stopped being jealous?"

"Oh, yes," said Maya. "I'm over all that. It was bliss while it lasted, but—"

"You said it hurt!" *And* she'd said he loved her back, which had quite obviously all been in her mind. "You said it hurt *so much.*"

"It did," said Maya. "It really did! But that's all part of it. You can't have love without pain. Like poor Jake and Miss Hopwood... It's so cruel!" She looked at me, with tears in her eyes. "Think how they must be suffering!"

"You reckon they were actually in love?"

"They must have been, or they wouldn't have gone off together! That day we bumped into them in the shopping centre... I could just tell," said Maya. "I knew there was something between them. That's why I got upset when you had a go at me... cos I *knew.*"

I said, "Really?" Obviously not sounding very convinced. Which wasn't surprising since I didn't believe a word of it. She hadn't mentioned *that* when she'd been crying and claiming he loved her!

"Honestly," said Maya. "It was obvious! You can always tell when people are in love. Well, I can," she said. "I can recognise the signs."

Meaning: she could but I couldn't. I am too boring and down to earth. To be honest I was still in two minds whether to believe the rumour or not, but later in the day we passed Jake in the main corridor. He was with a bunch of other Year Twelves so he wouldn't have said anything in any case, but normally he might perhaps have given us a smile or a nod. Today he didn't do either. Even to me, boring and down to earth though I am, it was obvious he wasn't happy.

"That's because he's heartbroken," said Maya.

I asked Mum, when I got home, whether she knew anything.

"Oh, so you've heard," she said. "I suppose it was

bound to get out. Yes, Jake's poor mum has been distraught. All she had was a text telling her not to worry, but how could she help it? No idea where he was, no idea who he was with, no idea when he was coming back."

"Mum, he was in love," I said.

Mum sighed. "Love can really cast a spell, especially at that age. Though I must say I was a bit surprised… Jake has always seemed so sensible."

Like me. I always seem so sensible. But it seems that even sensible people can sometimes have spells cast over them.

A year has gone by since the day Maya fell off her bike and got swept into Jake's arms, and so far she hasn't developed any more crushes. Maybe this is because Uncle Kev has been at home and she is starting to feel a bit more secure. This is what Mum thinks. Uncle Kev has promised faithfully that he isn't ever going to go away again, and this time it really does sound like he means it. Dad gives a hollow laugh, but that is just Dad.

Needless to say the doggy hotel for pampered pooches never came to anything, but Uncle Kev has had another brilliant idea that he is working on. He is digging up the whole of his back garden and is going to plant vegetables all over it and sell them to the local minimart (where Maya once sighed over Anil). Unfortunately his garden isn't very big so he is talking, if things work out, of taking over our garden as well. Dad says, "Over my dead body," but Mum just laughs and says she doesn't think he needs to worry.

At school we have a new music teacher, Mr Flinders. He is quite nice, but rather odd looking and not very young, so I don't think there is much danger of anyone running away with him. Miss Hopwood never did come back and nobody, not even Linzi, seems to know what has become of her. Jake, on the other hand, is away at uni and according to Mum, according to Mrs Harper, he has a lovely girlfriend of his own age.

Maya swears that she is not in the least bit jealous. She says all that is behind her, and that in any case when you have loved someone you should want them to be happy. She insists that what she felt for Jake wasn't just a crush but real true love. She also insists that you can't *choose* who to fall in love with.

"It's not something you have any control over. It just happens."

I can't help thinking that is a bit inconvenient if it leads you to fall in love with totally unsuitable people, but I don't say this to Maya. She would only accuse me again of being unsympathetic. Maybe, she tells me kindly, I will discover for myself one day. Maybe *I* will fall in love and then I won't be so quick to condemn.

I don't say anything, cos I'm not yet sure, but I suspect I might already be in the throes... We went up to Sheffield again a few weeks ago and Owen was there and I got the feeling he's definitely interested in me. We've been texting like crazy ever since I got back and now I can't stop thinking about him! It's not in the least bit painful so perhaps it is not yet real and true and that is still to come, but I am beginning to understand a little better how Maya was for ever walking round looking all dreamy with her head in the clouds and this soppy smile on her lips.

Not that I intend to have any soppy smiles. I think it would look silly with my sort of face, all round and freckly. But Dad did have to snap his fingers at me the other day and cry, "Hey! Dolly Daydream! I'm talking to you."

I hadn't heard a word he said! So maybe I am not quite as sensible and down to earth as Maya accuses me of being. She is not the only one who can fall in love!